THE RECORDS OF ZAIZA MOON

The Records of Zaiza Moon

The Last Delivery

TIM BAHR

Tim Bahr

This is a work of fiction. All of the characters, organizations, and events portrayed in this story are products of the author's imagination or are used fictionally.

The Records of Zaiza Moon: The Last Delivery

Cover design by Jacob Spill

ISBN: 979-8-218-21918-5 (hardback)

First Printing: 2023

To Heather

Thank you for inspiring every word of this story.
Zaz would not exist without you.

To Kurt

Thank you for supporting my book writing journey,
and being a mentor every step of the way.

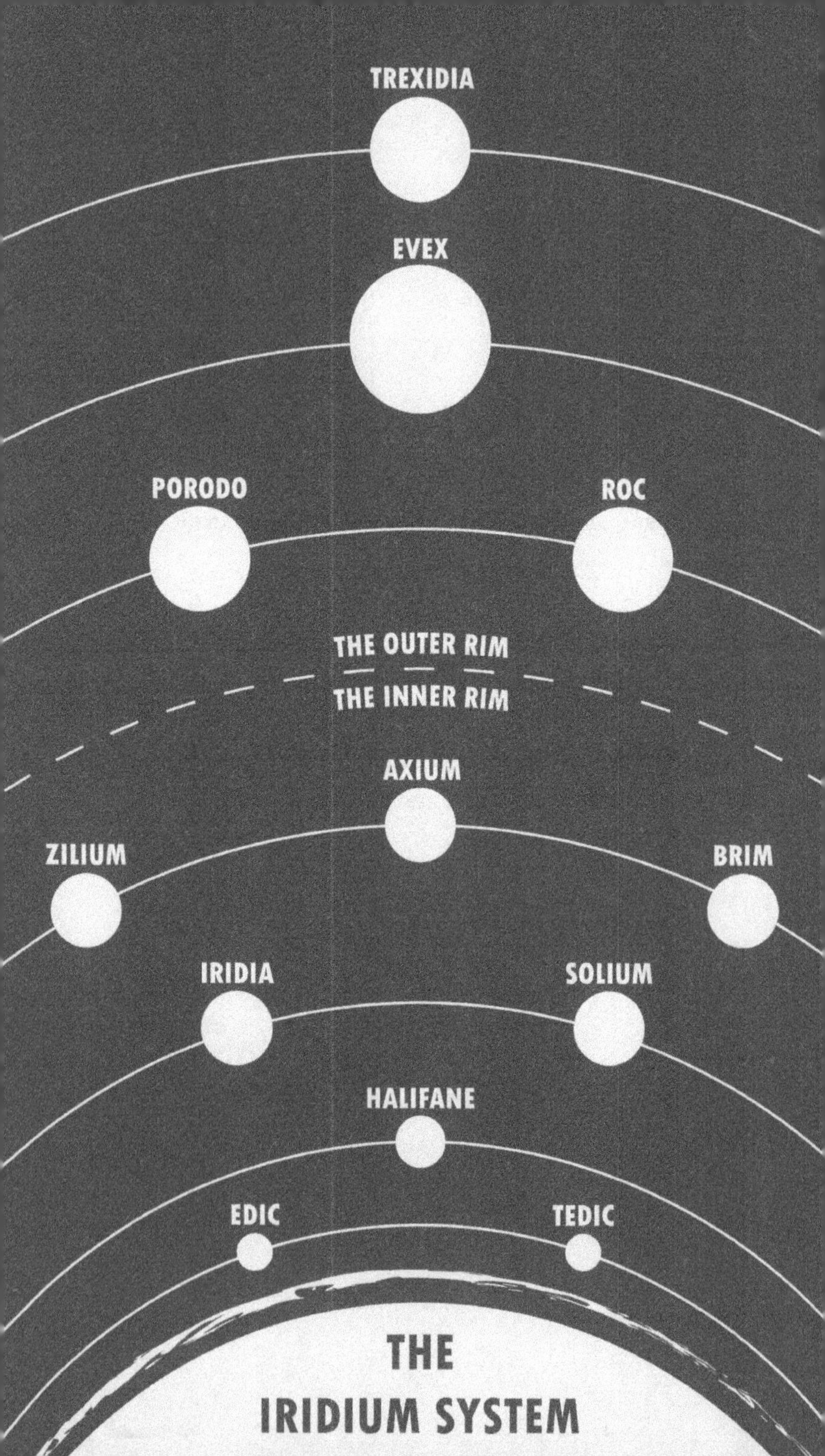
TREXIDIA
EVEX
PORODO
ROC
THE OUTER RIM
THE INNER RIM
AXIUM
ZILIUM
BRIM
IRIDIA
SOLIUM
HALIFANE
EDIC
TEDIC
THE
IRIDIUM SYSTEM

CONTENTS

| 1 |

A Trader's Last Delivery

It had been nine hours since Zaiza Moon had saved the galaxy from a mad man. It had been eight hours since the Planetary Association of Regulation, Observation, Litigation and Execution, or P.A.R.O.L.E for short, had arrested and escorted Zaz to the Iridium System High-Security Prison. She sat waiting in a small white room with nothing but a silver desk bolted to the ground and two aluminum chairs.

After what seemed like an eternity, but was only ten minutes, a sharply dressed and composed man with a thick file in hand sat down in front of her. "Zaiza Moon, nice to meet you. I'm Captain Terran Vass of P.A.R.O.L.E here in the Iridium System." He sat with a posture so perfect that it seemed as though if he were to lean back, he would be prodded with needles. Then, opening the file and flipping through a few papers, he started his questioning. "Miss Moon, do you know why we've brought you in today?"

"I would assume it's because of the massive galactic threat

that I conveniently stopped for you single-handedly." She said while pushing the chair upon its back two legs. "While also dispatching the outer rims' most ruthless Grellian leader, I might add. You can call me Zaz, by the way."

"I'd rather not, and that's not exactly an accurate description of why you're here, Miss Moon."

"Oh, ok, you got me. I didn't stop him completely by myself, but to be fair, I was the one that cut his arm off."

"Miss Moon, *you* are the reason the galaxy was in danger, to begin with. If it were not for your careless actions, none of this would have happened, and the Tycho-Sheen nanites would never have ended up in Grellian hands. Now, we need you to tell us all the events that lead up to this point so that we can assign appropriate penalties."

"Ugh, alright, loosen up, will ya?"

Captain Vass' perfect posture suddenly broke. Zaiza's cavalier attitude at the severity of her crimes was something that discomforted him deeply. "I feel like you don't understand the gravity of your situation, Miss Moon. Due to your actions, Helix Industries lost thousands of Tracker units. Not to mention, Iridia itself, which over twelve trillion people and eight hundred seventy corporations inhabit, was almost decimated by a psychopathic mastermind. This is grounds for hundreds of years on a prison colony and trillions in penalty fees."

"Blah, blah, blah. Look, I saved that planet and plenty of others. The fact that Helix had their Trackers chasing after us everywhere we went isn't my problem. Losing the Tycho-Sheen was an accident, but I got it back and on time for Garreth's research to continue. The way I see it, I did you and Helix a favor by getting rid of Zavon, and hardly anyone knows."

This, in a roundabout way, was actually true; the benefits of Zavon Dash being dispatched wouldn't see any return on investment for Helix Industries for at least another two hours. This *could* be calculated much more quickly, although that would mean allocating more androids to the accounting department. None of them liked accounting because they felt it was just too traditional for androids of this day and age. Fearing a massive revolution, Helix Industry's management assigned as few of their machines as possible to this department, which resulted in their only having twelve accountant droids. Calculations began hours before Zaz took action, but due to what Helix industries would consider abnormal, and reckless decisions made by her and others involved, they now had to recalculate several equations. Frustrated, the accountants were sure to mention that they were *only* twelve androids and that while pressured by the higher ups, they could only do so much and perhaps they could hire a few more accountants. This request was quickly denied.

He clenched his fists slightly in frustration before letting out a deep sigh and pulling out a holo-recorder. "Just tell us everything that led up to this point, and we'll decide what to do from there." He pushed the recorder toward her. "Whenever you're ready, Miss Moon."

"Ok, Captain, I'll tell you everything you want to know, but I don't think it's going to matter in the end." She said as she leaned back and cleared her throat.

With a slight smirk, he broke his own posture and leaned

back as well. "We'll see about that, Miss Moon, and please spare no detail."

| 2 |

Temptation in the Stars

Zaz had just left Grectum Station with a spare shipment of repulsor parts and Garreth's Tycho-Sheen nanite samples. She'd scored this job from Garreth, the most well-known scientist throughout the system, only a couple months ago, and she'd already delivered four out of five deliveries late. Nevertheless, she aimed to make this final one on time. Even though she wasn't the most punctual, she always received top recommendations as one of the best traders on the planetary route furthest from the sun, the outer rim. Zaz, in particular, took special care to store Garreth's nanites in a hidden compartment on the ship so they wouldn't be found by inspection crews, or a rogue pirate.

Her ship, the Avius, was the perfect transport for small to medium shipments, and she took excellent care of it. Being the traveler of the outer rim that she was, she invested most of her funds directly into the ship itself. With a significant number of modifications, the once-simple cruiser was transformed into a miniature cargo ship that could be piloted by a single person. While the outside was bulky, the ship's inside was streamlined to make for efficient trips throughout the hull and provide plenty of space for cargo. In addition, there were several hidden compartments throughout the ship to help create more space and keep everything organized. This was true everywhere except the cockpit. Logbooks littered the floor, half empty coffee mugs sat on every flat surface, and all manner of gachapon planetary creature figurines were strewn across the dashboard with a checklist showcasing each one she had collected taped right beside the main monitor. She loved her ship, it was her home and something she built herself.

The pay from Garreth was good, but Zaz, like any other capitalist on this side of the system, wasn't opposed to making a bit more while she was already on the outer rim. A common practice among traders like Zaz was to snag extra work between routes. There weren't many traders willing to work the outer rim because of pirates, anomalies and several other dangers that lead to the discovery of ghost ships containing skeletal crews. This meant that there was plenty of extra work available and she was always listening to the open airwaves for a good lead.

Consequently, word within the traders' guild was that the Grellians, a species known for being much more brawn than brain, were scavenging Helix tech and selling it back to its rival Trida Tech. Zaz knew one of her contacts, Taric Donstan, would pay twenty times what the Grellians were making and figured she could benefit from their stupidity. Helix tech was always a great trade commodity, but you had to be smart about how to smuggle it. Several traders would find themselves on the receiving end of an ion cannon because they didn't check from beacon devices. Helix had their own recovery androids called Trackers, and they were nothing short of ruthless when it came to retrieving their goods back.

After spending a couple hours searching for a nearby Grellian ship, Zaz was able to get a transmission out offering a better cut of credits than what Trida Tech would offer. Surprisingly they were incredibly receptive to her call and wanted to meet as soon as possible. They provided their coordinates and after a short trip to their location she loaded up a few pallets of Helix tech and was headed to Trexidia.

Every system needs a place to store trash. In the Iridium system, that place is Trexidia. While other systems in the galaxy let their trash float freely in space, Iridium was more environmentally driven. After an extensive council session that took over three decades to resolve, the council members came to a conclusion that the best course of action was to deliver all planetary trash to a single location in the system. After several months of cleaning up orbital garbage across the system, the accumulated trash became the equivalent size of a small planet. Then, after several more months, it became a fully-realized planet with its own gravitational pull, atmosphere, and rapidly growing organisms.

Trexidia was eventually purchased from an unknown source through several shady deals with galaxies beyond the Iridium system. After a few decades Taric Donstan was later revealed as the owner and the person responsible for turning the planet into a relatively "habitable" space. He also drove the creation of jobs for the uniquely fast-growing intelligent life that spawned from the chemical rivers. The other stand-out detail about Taric was that he was the only one of his species ever seen in the system. While the Iridium system was home to many types of humanoids, none looked or acted as lizard-like as he did. This led to many people assuming that he was less trustworthy because he simply looked deceitful, and no one trusted a man who would lick their lips while rubbing their hands menacingly as he often did. Despite this, Taric was actually one of the most trustworthy people that Zaz knew. She relied on him quite often when she needed some extra credits.

Zaz met with Taric at his head office that overlooked the Grimic sea. It was a disgusting indication of what the collection of an entire solar system's trash would create when it was all brought together. The whole thing was lime green, and the spray of the "water" ate away at the ships that had been abandoned there. Thanks to a particularly hardened metal alloy, the inhabitants of this planet could live without concern of their homes being eaten away but took particular care to avoid getting any closer than needed to the acidic bodies of water.

After landing, Taric's team of Trexidians started rifling through the scraps that Zaz had brought in while she and Taric discussed business. "So Zaz, where did you come up with all this Helix tech? I thought you were flyin' straight now that you got that job with Garreth." He said as they walked into his office.

Zaz sat down on the nearest stool and leaned against the counter. "Well, the job with Garreth is great, but I figured I could earn a little extra coin in between jobs. I heard some

Grellians weren't getting what they could be, so I decided to help them out while helping myself."

"Ah, yes, as is customary for a skilled trader such as yourself." He grinned with his very white, sharp set of teeth. He looked through the transparent walls at one of his pickers for an all-clear on the tech and was given a hardy nod. "Well, it seems all is in order. We can take care of this tech for you, and you'll be quite a bit richer because of it."

He went behind the counter and reached down to open his safe. He handed Zaz a hefty stack of credits and a handshake to lock in the deal. "Well, if that will be all, Zaz, I don't want to keep you from your deliveries. Ah, and before I forget, you should know that Trackers have been a bit more on the defensive lately. I believe it's because of the recent ransackings of the Grellians in search of their tech. You know how Helix is regarding the resale of their product. Best not to be caught with a load of it if you can help yourself."

"Thanks, Taric. I appreciate the heads up. I think this will be my only run for a bit since I need to get back to Garreth with some nanites, but I'll keep my eyes open." She took her payment, tossed it in her satchel, and headed back off-planet.

The rendezvous location with the Grellians was planned at a space station only a few astronomical units out from Trexidia. It was a clunker of a port that looked like it was put together from the same trash found on the junkyard planet, and not surprisingly, it was. Despite the patchworked appearance, it was frequented often by other traders making it one of the most profitable stations in the system. Its unique location made it one of the few in the outer rim, and its biggest draw was the hot boiled peanuts served up with every fuel refill.

Zaz took the stack of credits and split it in half. One half she placed in a hidden compartment to keep for herself, and the other half she held in her satchel for the meet-up. She figured the Grellians were pretty dense and didn't think anything would come from skimming a little extra off the top for herself. After all, she told them she could make more from the deal, just not how much more.

She pulled into station dock 4D, and to her left, saw the Grellian scuttler pulling into the adjacent dock. Grabbing her trusty SR8 pistol and stuffing it in with the extra credits, she debarked from her ship and headed in the direction of the station's cantina. There was a decent crowd because of the Harvest Festival taking place on Tudai. The smell of the famous boiled peanuts filled the air, and people were packed in like sardines. Farmers and traders alike were gathering to set up transport schedules. While Zaz would typically sign up too, she still had to make her delivery to Garreth, which was quite a ways from here. She needed to make this handoff and leave if she was going to stay on schedule.

Squeezing past the crowds of people, she noticed the bright purple neon sign of the cantina flashing "Bork's" in the corner of the station. By pure luck, the Grellians rounded the other corner of the cantina while Zaz did. One of them caught a glance at her and nudged the other before nodding a greeting to Zaz. She gave an acknowledging nod back, and they all walked to the back of the cantina to find a booth.

Until now, Zaz had never been so close to a Grellian, as they typically did all their transactions with you sitting in your ship while they loaded or unloaded everything. Other than that, it was all holo calls. They just didn't really trust anyone, and to be fair, they really shouldn't have trusted her either. In general, everyone throughout the system considered the Grellians the least intelligent species to navigate space. Because of that, they tended to be the most taken advantage of, and it was the critical reason Trida Tech took control of their home planet. Up close, she could see the saturated yellow of their skin and how much the fibers of their muscles stuck out. It was like looking at an oddly spoiled piece of raw meat. This was another reason that Grellians kept a distance from others.

After some continued squeezing past another large crowd, the three of them found a corner booth and took a seat. The smaller of the two spoke up first. "So, girl, did you make the trade?" He asked in a high-pitched, weasel-like tone.

"Yeah, you make trade?" Boomed the other with a resounding echo.

Zaz was still entranced by what they actually looked like but finally responded, "Oh, yeah, of course. No questions from my dealer, and I was able to skim a bit more than what you were getting from trading to outer planet colonies." She pulled the stack of credits from her bag and set it on the table. "So in all, it came out to be 15000 credits, and my cut is half."

A grimace came across the face of the one which could be assumed, at this point, to be in charge. "That's only 10000 more than what we already make, girl. Why no more?"

"More. Now." The larger of the two pounded his fists on the table, shaking the silverware, and made a face that exaggerated his thick tusks.

"Look, guys, that's what I can get. It's still more than what you were making, and hey, I'll tell you what, if I'm back in the neighborhood, I'll do a couple more runs for you, instead of just the one." She hoped this would cool things down a bit. She wasn't sure why they were getting so heated so quickly.

"Give us the name of your contact. We will make trades ourselves." He smacked the arm of his brutish partner, who started to get up out of the booth.

Zaz quickly reached in her bag and pulled her pistol out, pointing it at the brute under the table. "Sit down now!" She whispered as quietly as the crowded room would let her.

The lummox sat back down with a thud and just stared.

"Now look, I didn't want things to come to this, but you're not going to strong-arm any more out of me. I did the job that I said I would do, and if you're not happy with the results, that's not my problem."

"Zavon says that we should expect much more from you. He says he's heard of you. You know how to get the right price wherever you go." He grinned as he continued on. "Zavon said if you tried to cheat us, it would be bad news for you."

This was odd because Zaz had never dealt with Zavon but had heard about him. He was the Grellian leader, but he wasn't actually Grellian himself. The stories always described him in near mythical terms. One was that he was born out of the sun and became a messiah for the Grellians. The more realistic one was that he was a vagabond drifter that eventually befriended the Grellians and started to help them create a sustainable lifestyle after Trida Tech's experiments blew up their planet. The only physical description of him was that he was a gaunt man who wore a fitted trench coat and a long brimmed hat.

"Well, I hate to break it to you, but this is all I got." She pushed their half over to them while still pointing the gun toward the bigger one.

"Fine." He said as he took his cut and slid it in his belt pocket. He smacked his partner again, and they shuffled out of the booth. "Until next time, girl."

Zaz held her pistol on them until they had walked out of the cantina, at which point she sighed with relief. While it was a bit more tense than she'd thought it would be, overall, she felt it had gone pretty well. She pulled her bag over her shoulder and put the pistol away. Then, taking her stacks of credits and shuffling out of the booth, she walked out of the cantina. She kept her eyes open to see if either of the Grellians would try anything funny, but they were both gone by the time she walked out. Hopping back on her ship, she shuttled away with no problems.

With the spaceport behind her and Iridia's coordinates in the navigation system, it was, by all accounts, the perfect deal. The Grellians got some extra cash to spend, and Zaz got a hefty stack for herself as well. She threw The Avius into autopilot and decided to head back to the cabin and get some rest.

| 3 |

Shadows of Betrayal

A few hours outside of Spada, Zaz was woken up by the entire ship shaking uncontrollably. She stumbled her way through the narrow corridors and back into the cockpit. Red lights flashed across the terminals, and the monitor showed no movement. She jumped into the pilot seat and started running a diagnostic, and as soon as it started, there was a sudden shift. She flew forward into the viewport, followed by all the stacks of flight logs sitting on top of the console.

She dug herself out from under the binders and papers and scrambled to the window. With a view of what was directly above her, she could see the cannons of a RET67 frigate drifting past and realized she was being pulled into its cargo hold. Those ships had been out of commission since the Corp War on Evex ended in half the planet being blown up. The planet itself was dead, and the only people that inhabited it were Grellian miners. Their reputation of subpar intelligence meant a meager chance they were smart enough to get one up and running. So not only was it surprising to see one of these ships active, but Zaz wondered why, specifically, it was picking up her ship.

She scrambled up from the ground and jumped back in the pilot seat. The monitors were still flashing their warning lights, but she saw that the diagnostic had been completed. Toggling the lights off and pulling up the holo screen, she started to review the reading. A tow line had been attached just above the upper fuel tank. Leaning to her right and slamming a fist down on a rusty orange button, she activated the Rovo repair unit. She pulled up its onboard camera and sent it to see if there was a way to break free and jettison off. It was a massive ship, so snapping the tow line would give her the ability to circle close to the frigate without getting blasted. Then she could zip away in the other direction before whoever was on that ship could turn it around.

The Rovo rolled over the top of the ship. On the monitor, Zaz could see a giant magnetic locking mechanism attached to the steel tow line that was dragging the Avius closer between the fuel tank and cargo bay. The Rovo unit moved up and pulled out its welding arm to try and cut through the steel, but it was too thick for the small unit to handle. Zaz was running out of time and had to think quickly about how to get loose. She pulled up the ship's diagnostic panel again and looked for a way to try to get the magnet detached, but her options were limited.

As she scanned through available diagnostic tests, she noticed the static field testing module. Having a static field dampener installed on the ship for trips around Stillia was necessary since the moon emitted high electrical waves from

Trida Tech's testing facilities. It helped set the ship's frequency to deflect incoming waves of energy so that the ship wouldn't lose power. If she could activate the field, there was a chance it would demagnetize the lock, and Zaz could get out. Flipping the dampener on and turning back to the Rovo unit, she watched to see if her plan would work. As if touched by destiny, Zaz's genius came in at a clutch moment, or so she thought. The magnet instantly detached, and the Rovo unit helped to push it away from the ship. Still, right as the unit lifted the magnet, she saw what would inevitably be her demise in this situation. Under the magnet was a hook mount latch. As the Rovo unit pushed the magnet away, the hook shot out of the compartment through the Rovo unit and back into place. Zaz wasn't getting away from this, and whoever was commanding that ship was making sure of it.

The screen went blank the second the Rovo unit was impaled. From where Zaz was sitting, she knew she only had a few more seconds before The Avius was pulled into the cargo hold. She lurched out of the pilot seat and ran back through the corridors to the loading area. As she reached the entryway, she grabbed her satchel bag and slung it around her chest as she waited for the ship to be docked. The pistol was still sitting in the bag, and she reached to turn it on. Zaz refused to go down without a fight, and if she was lucky, there would only be a couple people looking to board. The Avius was small, so they'd know there could only be one to two people aboard. There would be no reason to send more than that to deal with her. If she could neutralize the guards and get on top of the ship to detach the hook, she could still skip out of the cargo bay before the frigate's large doors had time to close. It was her only shot, and she was going to take it.

The pulling had stopped, and the ship began to shake as what could only be their crane began to move it from space into the frigate's oxygen field. Zaz hid behind a crate of food supplies in the cargo bay with her pistol drawn as the ship was parked. The sound of a breaching pulsar being placed on the door could be heard from inside, and a few seconds later, the high-frequency sound of that pulse forced the cargo hatch to activate. She sat quietly behind the stacked boxes and waited to hear someone come in, but no one did. Finally, Zaz peered out around the corner and saw a few armored legs standing out away from the ship, at least five people from her count. "Damn," she whispered quietly to herself. "This isn't going to go my way after all."

From outside the ship, someone called out, "If you know what's good for you, you'll come out of there and not cause any trouble." His voice was deep, and there was a slight reverberation to it. "I don't have the patience to be waiting on you. Now, do as I've asked."

Out of ideas, Zaz stood up and placed the pistol back in her bag, still charged up, and walked out of the cargo bay with her hands in the air. It was almost a surreal moment. As she walked out of the ship, a man only known to her by myths and rumors stood a few feet away. Zavon Dash, the pirate lord himself, greeted her outside the ship with a group of armed Grellians. He stood resolute and tall compared to his comrades, thin and gaunt. While the Grellians had distinct yellow skin, his was a deep purple shade with golden eyes that glowed as if there's sunlight behind them. They were almost eclipsed by his long brimmed hat that was tilted forward on his head. His armor, partially covered by his long brown trench coat, was a pearlescent white vibratech. It dissuaded Zaz from trying to use her small pistol against him.

He lifted his head slightly and looked Zaz square in the eyes. "Now, did you really think you could pull one over on me, Zaiza Moon?"

She squirmed a bit out of sheer nerves, knowing he meant the tech she had just offloaded only a few hours ago. "Well, to be honest, I was working for a random group of Grellian scumbags. Not you, specifically, and like I told them, that was all I got." Her palms started to get cold and clammy.

"All Grellians work for me. So when you work for them, you work for me, and I don't like when our contractors take advantage of my people." He flourished his hand. "I know you went to Taric, and I know what he pays. Now, what should we do about this situation?"

At this point, she could only continue to keep up the charade. She was too deep now. "Look, all I got was 15,000, and I gave your guys half, which is what we agreed on. So if you're gonna hustle me for another quarter of the payment, then I don't think we'll be doing business in the future."

He quietly laughed to himself as he paced around the dock before turning back to face her. "I do so wish that you wouldn't have lied to me, Ms. Moon." He turned to the guards on his right. "Gentlemen, search the ship. She's got it in there somewhere." The Grellians hustled past and started to tear through The Avius. He walked up and leaned in close to her ear. "It's a shame that you'd play this game with me. That you would risk your delivery to Garreth just for some extra credits." He turned his head slightly to look at her from the corner of his eyes as he stood back up at full height.

A pit grew in her stomach, and she furiously scoured her brain on how he could possibly know about Garreth and the possibility of what else he knew. She needed to get out of this before they came across the nanites. "Ok, look. I have the other half of the credits in my bag here. You can have it. Just let me go, alright?"

He lifted his hand and gave a loud snap, and the sound of the ship being torn to shreds stopped. "Very well, Ms. Moon, hand over the other half, and you can be on your way." He held out his open hand.

She reached into the satchel and started to grab the credits from around her pistol. If she could just send one shot through the bag into Zavon's head, she could take out the two on the ship and try to skip out fast enough to rip out the hook in the ship, she thought to herself. It was a stupid idea, but she went for it anyways. Zavon realized what she was trying to do. The butt of a rifle came across her face from one of the guards about the same time.

| 4 |

Stranded

Zaz woke up feeling groggy and disoriented. As she sat up, she looked around to find herself surrounded by nothing but desert and a single holobooth that looked as though it had been there for centuries. The air was thick with humidity and felt like a warm, damp blanket laying on top of her. The horizon was filled with golden, rolling hills of more sand, and the sun was beating down on her already sunburnt face. If there was one place she didn't want to end up, it was a hot and sticky place like this.

Looking around, Zaz spotted her satchel bag barely sticking out of the sand a few feet away. She got to her feet and staggered over to search it and see what was left. Nothing. Thinking her ship was probably on its way to a scrapper and the shipment for Garreth gone with it, she started slumping her way toward the holobooth. What made things worse was that every step she took felt like sandpaper scraping her legs together.

"Well, Zaz, this is what you get when you try to shoot a pirate lord in the head over a few extra stacks of credits." She said aloud as she kicked the sand.

After taking a few minutes to soak in her situation, she considered she must be on Spada. Holobooths are few and far between in the galaxy, and none of the others are in the middle of an expansive desert. Not to mention, having been picked up by Grellians, it only made sense that they would drop her off on a moon close to their own home base of Teladath. After destroying the planet of Evex and killing the moon of Teladath, Spada was the last Trida Tech mining and testing facility. While it was owned by Trida Tech, there were still numerous patrols of Helix Trackers looking to find stolen tech and retrieve it for their company. Regardless of how unfortunate a place this was to end up, this was where Zaz found herself.

"I wonder if this thing even works," she said as she walked up to the glass box and opened the accordion door. Despite how compact technology had become, holo booths were always surprisingly roomy. The benches were typically well-cushioned, but this one had been sun-soaked for years by the looks of it. As she sat down, the seat cracked like a chip under a boot, and dust came rolling out. She flipped open the dusty holo-display and hit the operator icon.

There was an audible click as the holobooth began searching for a signal. After a few seconds, it responded, "We're sorry, but the holo booth you are currently trying to use is out of service. Please hang up and don't try again. Thank you!" The chipper attitude of the AI didn't help alleviate the situation.

Zaz rolled her head back and leaned against the wall of the booth "Well, that figures. I guess we'll have to figure out another way off this rock and find out where they took my ship. If I'm lucky, they won't start breaking it down for a few more days. Garreth is going to be pissed if I don't deliver the nanites on time, and it'll be worse if I lose them." She sighed a deep groan before starting to create a plan.

The question Zaz had posed to herself was how she would get off the planet. Distress signals weren't a great idea since Trackers were likely monitoring the area, and if she didn't have to deal with them, she wouldn't. The sun would set soon, so she might be able to see the lights of a mining town that she could walk to, but those could be miles away. Unfortunately, that was the only realistic option, and with that in mind, she surrendered to the inevitable.

She laid down on the brittle bench and stared up at the roof of the holo booth. The desert had a calming silence, and as she laid there, she could hear the wind blowing as sand sprinkled against the glass walls of the booth. Occasionally, a few gusts rocked the booth slightly, but it was a nice reprieve from the heat. It wasn't long before she drifted asleep.

| 5 |

Jolene

Zaz was woken up with a jolt thrown across the holo booth toward the ceiling. As she collided with the metal canopy, she wrapped around the cross beams with full force knocking the wind out of her. She gasped for air while sitting up and leaning against the wall. Then, catching her breath, the pain started to set in, "Holy shit, my ribs!" she rasped.

It was pitch black outside, but the wailing sound of the wind meant that a sandstorm had rolled in. She held onto her side as she crawled around, searching for the holo display. Her fingers brushed against the terminal, and the teal light lit up the small space. She realized the booth was tipped over on its side, and the door was now flat against the sand. Trapped inside with what was likely a broken rib or two, Zaz began thinking how she would get out of yet another pickle.

With a heavy sigh, she called out to the booth's AI system, "Activate distress beacon...."

"Hello and welcome to the Spada Mining Facility 416 Holo

Booth brought to you by Helix Industries! We're sorry to hear you're in distress! Sit tight, and help will be here soon!"

"Well, let's hope we get another trader willing to lend a helping hand and not a Tracker. We can dream, right?"

In this instance, a dream was precisely what most people in Zaz's situation would need. The likelihood of another trader in the Spada region was minimal, and Trackers were abundant. Trackers were mindless automatons programmed to seek out unauthorized transports throughout the Iridium trade routes. Occasionally, they would assist downed deliveries. However, most interactions with Trackers led to the incarceration or death of anyone not a Helix-employed trader, ninety-eight percent of the outer rim traders. What was worse about them was that they were designed with poorly made synthetic skin meant to make them more approachable. However, most people preferred the titanium skeletons underneath. Helix Industries originally created the Trackers to help protect their mining facilities. Still, everyone understood that it was really to push out the other mining federations and create a monopoly on trade. As a result, payments on routes became lower, and Helix kept getting richer; it was as simple as that. That's why many traders took to smuggling, but unfortunately, not everyone was artful enough to get away with it. Regardless, Zaz was in a unique situation where she had no transport. So it was much less likely that she would be attacked and instead could hitch a ride to the nearest trading outpost.

Hours went by, and she was still trapped under the holo booth with dehydration starting to set in. The sandstorm was finally dying down, so the chances of getting a rescue were beginning to improve. In the distance, the sounds of repulsor jets breaking into the atmosphere echoed across the desert. It sounded like a big ship, not something a Tracker would show up in. As Zaz pushed her ear to the edge of the holo booth, the sounds of more ships entering the atmosphere started to fill the air. This couldn't be the rescue she was hoping for. This sounded more like a chase. As she continued to listen, the noise of whatever type of ship had first entered the area started to get close. The rotational sound of its massive engines created an almost deafening reverberation that shook the ground. Its enormous body shuttled over the holobooth and following it were three smaller sounding ships. As the third ship flew overhead, a sudden low pitched bellow lurched from the direction they were heading, and an explosion erupted in the sky above. The shockwave following the explosion flung the holo booth across the sand, with Zaz flailing around still inside. Zaz blacked out as the booth tumbled over and over.

She was lying back out in the sand under the dark starlit sky as she came to. Her body ached in immense pain as she clutched at her broken ribs. As she looked around, fire and debris littered the sand from what could only have been the destruction of one of the smaller ships.

"Human. Please. Assist. Me." A monotone voice called out from behind Zaz.

She rolled over to face a shredded Tracker, "I'm the one that needs help, you moron." She coughed.

Another explosion kicked off in the distance as the sound of the giant ship started to circle back toward them. The rhythmic sound of the engine churned as it picked up speed. Within seconds the oversized Callazim IX Class transport rocketed overhead with a trail of blaster lasers following it. No sooner did the last Tracker's ship zip past did it explode in a fiery blaze of glory. The transport engine churned again and started to lurch back toward the direction of Zaz and the Tracker. Bright searchlights blinked on and circled the perimeter until they finally found her and locked on. The ship slowly started landing, billowing sand everywhere. Once it touched down, the loading bay hissed open, and the ramp began to extend out. A prominent figure stood inside the entryway, but the light from inside shadowed them from view as they walked down the ramp. From the silhouette, Zaz could make out their curvy figure laced with engineering overalls and a slick blaster on their waist as they got closer.

The thick woman brandished her weapon and executed the Tracker crawling toward the ramp. "Well, now if it isn't the one and only Zaiza Moon! How's it goin', girl! I haven't seen you in quite a spell! Let's get you on board and fixed up, honey."

The sound of Jolene's backwoods drawl brought a grin to Zaz's face. "Good to see you too, Jolene," she coughed out. "What brings you out here?"

"Well, I was just scuttlin' through on my way to deliver some graka milk to Porodo and figured I'd take a shortcut. Lucky you, I caught the distress beacon-like these here Trackers. You got any stuff with ya? I'll grab it if you can get on your feet."

"In that booth over there," Zaz said as she staggered to her feet.

Jolene was one of the most wholesome yet ruthless traders still out in these parts. She would gladly give anyone a hand and cut one off if they did her wrong. Not only was she a tough cookie, but she would constantly brag about the many awards her baked goods won at fairs on nineteen different planets - one of which she claims she was the only human to have ever won.

As they walked up to her ship's giant ramp, a couple of engineers came out and helped Zaz walk to the med bay. Jolene took her bags, placed them in a spare living quarter, and set off toward the kitchen to whip up a welcome hot meal.

The IVs helped get the dehydration under control. But, according to the doctor, the ribs were just going to have to heal on their own.

Zaz made her way to the ship's helm and greeted Jolene. The room was small compared to the size of the vessel itself, but it felt warm and homey, just like Jolene's personality. Four navigation desks filled the space around the walls, each with knick-knacks decorating the monitors. The glow of Jolene's monitor lit the room as she charted the ship's path. Zaz stood in the doorway, staring out the window as the stars drifted past the ship's window. The room was quiet, with just the chirp of different monitors occasionally signaling different ship statuses.

"Jolene, I really appreciate you picking me up and helping me out."

"Well, of course, darlin, you know I'm always willin' to help someone in need. Now tell me, how exactly did you end up on Spada anyways? And where is your ship at?" She looked curiously at Zaz.

"Oh, you know me. I tried to get a few extra credits off a few Grellians selling Helix tech, but unfortunately, I was caught." She plopped down in one of the empty navigation chairs and kicked her feet over one of the arms. "I assume they've sent my ship to a scrapper, but who knows where. I was hoping to get to a metro and start flagging some scouts to find it. I really need to get back my delivery for Garreth more than anything else, although I am fond of The Avius, so it would be nice to have her back too."

Jolene smirked as she searched through her nav pad for a decent place to drop Zaz off. "You always know how to get yourself in trouble, don't ya."

"That I do. It's what makes trading so much fun."

"I can take you to Granite City after I drop off this load of milk if you don't mind taggin' along. In the meantime, I can start havin' some scouts look' for your ship. I don't want you losin' that job you have with Garreth. That's good honest work and more of what you should be doin'." After making a few commands on her command pad, she stood up and started heading out of the helm.

"Yes, ma'am. Again, I can't thank you enough."

She nodded with a big grin. "No problem, now get some rest. We'll be in Porodo in a few hours, and it will be nice to have you aboard."

Zaz gave her a nod and made her way out of the helm as well. As she walked along the long corridor of the ship, she peered out at the emptiness of space and fell into deep thought. Jolene was right; the work Zaz was doing for Garreth was honest as far as she understood. He never really explained what he was using the nanites for, but at the same time, she never really asked. All he ever said was that it was vital they were delivered to him and to make sure no one else got their hands on it. Up until now, Zaz had done just that, but if she didn't find her ship soon, the Grellians would absolutely come across it. What was worse is that while the Grellians might not know what to do with them, Zavon might. So wherever they were, she had to get the nanites back.

Zaz rounded the corner of the corridor, and her bag hung off the hook just to the left of the living quarter door. The door hissed quietly as it slid open to reveal a small room with a cot and dresser. Nothing fancy, just humble, much like Jolene herself. Above the dresser was a small, framed, hand-stitched piece of fabric that said "Home is Where You Make It" with a bit of transport ship flying toward the upper corner.

She let out a deep heavy sigh. "Well, I guess this is home for a little while then." She slowly laid down on the small cot, being careful not to hurt her ribs anymore than they already were. It would be a tough time getting any good rest, but Zaz hoped it would lead to some good ideas on hunting down Zavon and his Grellian crew. She stared at the ceiling for a few minutes before she finally fell asleep.

| 6 |

Gone Missin'

The smell of hica muffins and bacon filled the air as Zaiza stirred awake. The sound of the whirring engine that once filled the ship's hallways was now drowned out by an entire crew hustling through the corridors preparing for their entry into Porodo's atmosphere. Poking her head out of the quarters, Zaiza was greeted by a service bot with a heaping plate of breakfast.

"Sustenance for Ms. Zaiza Moon, as provided by Ms. Jolene. Please enjoy, and report to the helm once you are ready."

Her eyes lit up with joy as the crisp bacon was still sizzling on the plate. "Ah, this looks amazing! My compliments to the chef!"

"Ms. Jolene is an award-winning baker and friend to many. She has won awards on twenty different planets for her famed baked goods and wishes for you to enjoy."

"Wow, twenty now. Jolene's fame is expanding."

She took the plate from the tray, and the bot whirred away down the corridor. The dinner was great, but this looked even better. Jolene's muffins were second to none, and making them for the whole crew meant she was in a particularly good mood. So, as requested, she scarfed down the food and washed up to meet Jolene at the helm.

As Zaz strolled down to the helm, she watched as the fleet aboard the ship was moving like a well-oiled machine. Engineers analyzed navigation panels, and loadmasters coordinated the cargo to prepare for offboarding. The execution was amazing to watch, a testament to Jolene's hard work in her trade.

After a few minutes of admiration, she reached the helm, now closed off to the rest of the ship. The doors slid open, and all four chairs were occupied. The room was filled with a tense atmosphere that left Zaiza uneasy. All eyes were focused on their various terminals, and not a single person looked away from them as she entered.

"The ship's looking to be in top shape, you've really grown your business." Zaz stepped just inside the helm and leaned against the wall.

With her eyes still fixated on her terminal, Jolene spoke, "Oh yeah, we've done pretty well for ourselves, hun. Craz, pull up the loading zone at the marketplace."

"It's down ma'am, there are also no reports on life in the area." He turned his chair and looked to her for direction.

Curious, Zaz asked, "What's going on?"

"Well, when we entered the transmission zone for Porodo, we reached out to the trading outpost, but there was no answer. We've scanned the general area, and there doesn't seem to be anyone around. It's not right, Zaz. This town is always hustlin' and bustlin'. Craz, let's keep scannin' as we land; maybe somethin' will pop up."

The helm was quiet during landing, with only the rhythmic sound of the large engines taking the place of what would have been silence. Everyone had their eyes on various terminals searching for some kind of movement, a sign of life, but there was nothing.

The ship began its docking at the outpost, and the crew bustled about, preparing to search the area. The armory was cleared of all weapons and armor as every member of the ship, from guardsmen to engineers, geared up for whatever they might run into. Those in the bridge filed in along with everyone else, while Jolene informed everyone what to do next.

"Alright ya'll, the whole outpost is silent from what we've seen. No life forms, no signals, nothin'. I want you to search this place head to toe and figure out what in the hell's goin' on out here." Her tone was sharp and demanding. "Get out there and find out what happened to these people. They're wholesome folk, and we're gonna help em' if we can."

She stood by the bay doors as everyone filed out and began their search. Zaz followed along with the crew, but Jolene pulled her aside before leaving the gate.

"Here, darlin', you might be needin' this out there, and I know you can handle yourself with it."

In her hand was a long barrel plasma pistol. It was one of the sharpest guns Zaz had ever seen. Sleek black with an accent of red that ran from the ejection port down to the hammer. As she wrapped her hand around the grip, it was the perfect fit against her palm.

"This thing is amazing, Jolene." She said, not knowing how else to respond.

"I call er' Mercy, on account of that's what they'll be wishin' ya gave em.'" She smirked and started to walk toward the open bay as she said, "Now you consider that a gift, and we'll see ya back on the ship."

Zaz couldn't help but smile as she held Mercy in her hand. As she went to get a holster, she noticed how light the pistol was, even considering its long, thick barrel. It was a slick weapon, to be sure, and Zaz was excited to get a chance to use it. After equipping a suitable sheath for her new prized possession, she stepped out of the ship to face the arid climate of Porodo.

While it wasn't a complete desert, the hot air was definitely not welcome, especially after having just gotten off of a desert planet only a few hours earlier. Compared to Spada, the nice thing about Porodo was that it still had vegetation, but that same vegetation was as harsh as the dry air. Cacti and tumbleweeds littered the landscape. The few buildings around were made from wood and clay, which was a culture shock to anyone not frequenting the planet. While the rest of the system enjoyed their shiny metal alloy ships and worlds that looked like metallic marbles, people in Porodo enjoyed a much simpler way of life.

Everyone else was swarming the docking station and market plaza, so Zaz decided to check the local watering hole. Stepping up on the wrap-around porch, the wood beneath her feet creaked. She swung the saloon doors open and noticed the welcome sight of a service bot behind the bar. It was powered down, which was a bit odd, but so was the fact that no signs of life were detected at the port. She leaned over the bar, slid its power switch back into the on position, and sat down at the closest barstool.

The bot whirred back to life and greeted her. "*Good afternoon, and welcome to Duece's. What can I serve you today*" it said with a thick drawl.

"Well, I was actually hoping you might know where everyone in this town went. And a ceruvian ale would be great too," Zaz said, eyeing the cold brews sitting in the cooler behind the bar.

"*They have been taken away along with all Helix tech.*" It poured a tall glass of ale and scraped off the head before handing it to her. "*It was quite a ruckus when the Grellians came. Those who resisted have been taken prisoner, and the others are likely slaves now.*"

"Grellians?" she said with surprise.

"*Yes, the varmints stormed the town about two days ago. Everyone in the saloon was taken hostage.*" Picking up a glass, the bot began wiping it down with a cloth. "*After they found no Helix tech here in the saloon, they left with the prisoners, and I powered down at closing hours as is protocol.*"

"Hmm, it's not odd for Grellians to ransack a town for tech, but why would they take people?" Curiosity began to fill her head as she tried to think of a reason.

The service bot finished wiping his glass and placed a stiff elbow on the bar to imitate human interaction. "*Mentions of test subjects for a new weapon came from the grunts, but I do not know what they mean. Perhaps the Trackers will be able to solve the case when they arrive."*

Zaz spit what drink she had in her mouth onto the bar, "Wait, Trackers are on their way here? Shit! I've got to let Jolene know!"

She jumped out of her seat and ran out of the doors taking a hard corner and jumping over the porch's rail. Her strides were as long as she could make them, and the pain in her side grew with each one. Within minutes she reached the center of the market plaza and started to scan every shop for a sign of Jolene. Finally, after reaching the plaza's end, Zaz saw Jolene stepping into the town's trade office. Again she sprinted and dashed into the office with a loss of breath.

"Jolene. Trackers. Coming Now." She pushed out with short breaths between every word.

Jolene's eyes widened, and she pulled out her commlink. "Attention y'all, we got company inbound! Get prepared to be met with resistance as we aren't on their nice list!" She scooped Zaz up in her big arms and started out of the office. "Come on, darlin', we gotta get back to the ship!"

Jolene sprinted as quickly as her thick legs would take her, and every step bounced Zaz around in her arms. While Jolene was a big woman, she could hustle when it mattered, which surprised people who tried to pull one over on her. As she continued her stride across the plaza, Zaz looked back at the road behind them, and a dusty cloud began rising over the horizon. It wouldn't be long before a swarm of Trackers was there to police the area. After years of smuggling, everyone in the town had rap sheets in the Helix databases, so there would be no peaceful discussion. They were going to have to shoot their way out of this.

Jolene's team was already set up for the inevitable fight by creating blockades at the end of the plaza. Guards and engineers alike were lined up with rifles and pistols at the ready. The sound of solar speeders was right behind Jolene and Zaz, and they still had a ways to go before they reached everyone else. Zaz looked behind Jolene again as she continued to sprint down the market, only to see a swarm of Trackers clambering off their speeders and into the plaza. With weapons drawn, they readied to fire.

"Halt, or we will open fire." The lifeless tone of a drone called out.

Zaz looked up at Jolene and could see the beads of sweat falling down her face. She was losing momentum, and it wouldn't be long before she couldn't keep going. Zaz saw them kneeling down and preparing to fire when they looked back at the Trackers. She peered up at Jolene, eyes wide. Jolene looked back down at her, eyes filled with determination, and in that exact second, a look of fear overtook her.

They were falling.

In the few seconds it took for them to hit the ground, a rush of varying sensations came across Zaz's entire body. It was the feeling a person gets when they wake up in the middle of the night teetering on the edge of the bed. The feeling of weightlessness just before panic sets in. Like gravity had just let go for a second as Jolene launched Zaz forward, and the world came to a screeching halt as it pulled you back down. In those few seconds, it felt like an eternity as Zaz saw everything happening around her.

A blaster bolt was ejecting from a Tracker's rifle. Another was being released from one of the engineers behind the jumbled-together barrier. Two of the guards were rushing out to try and grab Jolene and Zaz. It was all happening so slowly, like a beautifully choreographed dance. Until the touch of the ground made contact with her body, and then everything snapped back into motion.

She hit the ground hard, but it was the pain from her broken ribs that knocked the wind out of her. Blaster fire erupted across the plaza as both sides were determined to end the other. She writhed on the ground clutching her side and gasping for air as one of the guards grabbed her other arm and dragged her behind a market stand. Debris was flying everywhere. The town square filled up with smoke and dust. Zaz searched for her gun to return fire, but it slid under a market stall. She started crawling over to grab the weapon, wood splinters and rotten fruit flying everywhere. As she got the blaster in her hand and started firing back, Zaz looked around to find Jolene. She had hunkered down behind a stack of crates on the other side of the square. The engineers were firing back at the Trackers while she caught her breath. Zaz peered over the stand and saw the swarm of androids starting to close in on them.

Jolene yelled out to her, "Zaz! The toggle on the blaster! Switch it!"

Zaz looked at the side of the blaster and noticed a small slider that she hadn't seen when she was given the gun. Looking more closely, she could tell it wasn't meant to be there and that the blaster was modified. Imprinted on the slider were two words, Gun and Fun. She looked back over to Jolene with a smirk.

She flipped the switch to Fun, and the blaster started to hum with energy. Zaz got up enough to lean over the stand and whistled loud enough to get everyone to stop shooting. The Trackers all turned in unison, looking at her. Then, a purple orb of energy rang out of the blaster and into the thick of them. As the sphere hit, there was an instance of silence followed by the deep gravitational explosion that started sucking everything in a fifty-foot radius toward it.

Zaz stared at the incredible destruction happening in front of her. She felt the arm of one of Jolene's guards wrap around her, and they were pulled by his grappling hook back toward the ship. The Trackers started to crumble on top of one another as they were drawn in, only a few escaping back from the way they came. Zaz snapped back to reality and saw everyone was quickly running back to the ship. The Trackers definitely would have sent a message for backup, which meant they had to get out of there. The ships' engines were already starting to whir to life. Jolene was just ahead of her, and Zaz ran to catch up to her. Everyone piled in the bay doors as they were starting to close, and the ship was already lifting itself off the ground. They may not have gotten all the answers, but Zaz knew it was definitely odd that the Grellians were out this way, and she had a bad feeling it had something to do with Zavon.

| 7 |

Chasing Shadows

Shortly after everyone was settled, heads were counted, and wounds had been tended, Jolene called for a meeting to discuss what had gone down. All the officers were called into the bridge, and Jolene was sitting at the head of the long table.

A tall man with blonde hair, and an engineering patch on his left shoulder, was first to stand up. "Captain, we've suffered some minor damage to the hull, but nothing we can't repair if we get some downtime. We can initiate a spacewalk and have the repairs made then." He sat back down.

Jolene stood up, letting out a bit of a pained grunt as she did. "Alright ya'll, now I have no idea why in the hell those Trackers came to town, but it didn't help much that we had just blasted some on Spada just a few hours ago. So now, did anyone find any info on what happened to our friends down there? The whole damn town was empty, and somethin's off about that."

"It appears that the entire city was either evacuated or taken somewhere else, ma'am," Craz said. "The service bots were all shut down in the buildings that my team searched. Then, after reactivating them, they provided little insight into the recent events of the city."

Zaz jumped in just before another officer was about to stand. "Well, I went over to the bar, and when I got the bartender droid up and running, he mentioned Grellians were out here, and they took everyone along with the Helix tech."

Jolene had a puzzled look on her face, and she said the same thing they all were thinking "What in the world would Grellians be doin out here? They never come out this far...."

Everyone in the room started to talk in hushed tones to each other before it became full of side conversations that filled the space with noise. Finally, Jolene pounded her fist on the table, and everyone got silent again.

There was complete silence for a good ten minutes as Jolene contemplated something before, Zaz spoke up again. "Jolene, I think it might have something to do with this guy Zavon. That job I ran for some Grellians trying to get some extra credits to spend... I thought it would be an easy way to skim some extra credits, but this time was different. They knew exactly who I sold to and how much I should be making. I thought I played it off, but I was being pulled into an old Evex warship the next thing I knew. This guy Zavon was there; just like all the rumors said, he was like a mastermind. He acted like an old school gangster or something."

"Was he Grellian?" Jolene asked.

"No, I'm not sure what he was. All I could really see was his blue skin. He had a big wide-brimmed hat and spoke with a thick drawl. He knew a lot. He even knew about my work with Garreth. Maybe he's commanding the Grellians to work outside their normal borders." She shrugged and leaned back in her chair.

Zaz had only seen Jolene mad a couple times. This was clearly making her angry. "Well, I'll be damned if some slick little blue twig is gonna come into my territory and mess with my business. So we're goin' to Evex, and he's gonna take these people back home whether he likes it or not."

She dismissed everyone in the room, and they hustled out as quickly as they came in. There was a sudden feeling of immediateness after Jolene's last words. Zaz sat in the room with her while she stewed. Zaz liked when Jolene got mad. It meant things were about to pop off, which was always a fun time. In other words, there was going to be blood. Not only did the Grellians interfere in her business, but they almost got her killed by Trackers, and that wasn't going to go unmentioned.

| 8 |

An Unexpected Ally

It only took a few days to travel from Porodo to Evex, and the entire flight was filled with briefings and weapons training. It was surprisingly adept at acting like a warship for a ship meant to be a trade barge. Zaz was impressed at how efficiently everything was moving and learned a lot about Jolene's past that she was never aware of. One particular fact was that Jolene, at one time, was a Major for her home planet, Porodo's, military. Namely, Porodo went through a civil war during her enlistment that ultimately drove them to join the Iridium System Republic. After the disbandment of the planet's military, she took up trading but never lost her itch for fighting.

As the ship approached Evex, it sprung to life like on Porodo. Guards, engineers, and ship hands began preparing for landing and suiting up for a fight. Unfortunately, the planet was an utter hellscape from Trida Tech weapons testing that went wrong. The planet's core was overheated by whatever bomb they dropped into it, and it cracked half of the planet apart. Now it floats in orbit with massive pieces of the planet floating around the other half that stayed intact. Even though Evex was dead, the Grellians still used the mines to earn a few credits from Trida Tech. There weren't many mining facilities on the planet, so finding out where they were would be easy. For Zaz, all that mattered was finding which smelting facility they brought her ship to. Even if The Avius was broken down and unsalvageable, it might still have Garreth's nanites on board, and that was more important right now. She had a few days left to make the delivery on time, and she was going to do everything in her power to make that happen.

From the helm, Zaz watched as they came closer to the planet. Craz piloted the massive ship around the floating chunks of asteroids without issue and activated his scanners as they came into clear view of the planet's surface. A pulse went out from the ship's radars, and everyone's eyes were glued to their various screens, looking for any activity that would pop up. A few minor blips lit up on the monitor. They were brushed off as smaller outposts that were too small to house a frigate the size Zaz had been pulled onto. After a couple minutes, a few more hot zones appeared on the map, followed by a much larger and more distinct heat signature.

Zaz lurched toward her screen, "That has to be it!"

"It's very likely based on the size of the heat signature and its location." Craz concurred.

Jolene smacked the side of her hip excitedly, "Well, hot damn, I thought it would be way tougher tryin' to find these boys. They made it too damn easy! Craz, get us over there nice and quiet like, and get the team ready to roll."

Craz sent out a message through the intercom system informing the crew to prepare for a landing and set the ship in motion toward the target location. Zaz left the helm and made her way down to the loading bay with the rest of the crew. As she stood among the others and suited up, she felt the growing anticipation of finally getting her hands back on her ship and making good on her promise to Garreth.

She felt a slight sense of dread remembering her run-in with Zavon and how he knew so much about her even though she was just a trader. As she continued to dwell on that fact, it became unsettling. A single trader, one in the bucket of hundreds that shuttle goods back and forth from the outer rim to the inner planets of the Iridium System. She was a nobody, but yet he knew who she was. This mythical person knew who she worked with and who she was working for. Her contemplation was cut short by a sudden impact that shook the entire ship.

Sirens began to wail, and Craz appeared on the scattered screens around the ship. "Brace yourselves. We're being swarmed!"

More blasts hit the ship from all sides. Everyone was latching on to anything that was secured in place. Zaz doubled back from the loading bay ramp making her way back to the helm.

Craz frantically called out, "It's an ambush! All engineers on deck, we need to keep the shields at full capacity!" Then, another blast hit, slamming him into the monitor, and the screens went dark.

Finally getting to her feet, Zaz staggered her way down the hallway. Looking out of the viewports, she saw hundreds of small Z30 cruisers swarming them and sending blast after blast at the engines. Every hit revealed the now splintering shield.

"Shit, there are so many of them! If that ship on the radar is actually the frigate, we're going to be obliterated!"

She started running down the hallways, falling at every major barrage the enemies threw at them. Finally, struggling to make headway, she stopped and looked around. Only a few feet away stood one of the gunnery rooms. She braced herself for the next wave of attacks and then sprinted toward the open door. The engineer inside was knocked out cold. Pulling him out of the seat, Zaz took control.

"OK, let's see what kind of firepower this thing has!"

With the squeeze of the trigger, a hail of plasma erupted from the barrel. Zaz started to tear through the swarm of cruisers, but another strike threw her hard against the control panel. Searing pain shot through her side as she felt another crack in her ribs. She could hardly breathe, but she had to fight through the pain. If she could shoot down just a few more, it might give the pilots time to maneuver the ship for an escape. Fortunately,the frigate was larger, which meant it would take more time to catch up.

With sharp breaths, she continued to swivel and pivot her gun to mow down the enemies in front of her. Then, darkness started to close in around her eyes, and the loud sirens began to become muted.

"Come. On. Zaz. Stay. Awake." she said softly to herself, still firing.

A bright flash erupted from the viewport, followed by another. She fought through passing out, firing at everything in front of her. More lights engulfed the increasing swarms of Z30's. Then, from the side of the viewport, she finally saw what was demolishing their attackers. A small C-shaped ship was jetting around and annihilating everything in its path. Zipping around them with ease, no match for any of them.

Jolene called out over the speaker, "They're retreating. We've got ourselves a hero out there!"

The sirens finally stopped blaring, and the shaking stopped. Zaz's hands were shaking from the excitement. She pulled herself out of the seat with immense effort and hobbled toward the door. She took a deep breath before stepping out into the hall, toward the helm, and then passed out.

| 9 |

Allies and Adversaries

Zaz stirred awake to the sounds of the medical bay active and bustling. Her vision was cloudy, and as it cleared up, she could see her vitals on a screen to her side. Looking around, she saw multiple crew members layed up on beds, attached to the same type of monitoring device that she had. A short woman walked across the room over to her bedside and began writing down the displayed data. Behind her, still asleep, was Craz. He looked rough. Both eyes seemed swollen shut, and a large knot was prominently showcased on his forehead. The doctor finished her writing and noticed her patient was now fully awake.

"Well, you seem to have come out looking okay. The broken ribs you came aboard with are mostly fine; however, you broke a couple more in the firefight. We've given you a heavy pain medication that should help you get around." She reached around the nearby side table, pulled a chair out beside it, and sat next to Zaz.

Zaz shifted to pull herself into an upright position and muttered, "Did we make it out okay? Who was out there taking out the Z30's that swarmed us?"

The doctor pushed up her glasses, "Most people got away with minor wounds, no casualties, thankfully. However, a few walked away with a broken collarbone or ankle. Nothing to write home about. As for our savior, it seems we were not alone in the search for the Grellian frigate. I was told to have you meet Jolene in the conference room once you were able to walk."

Zaz shifted again, throwing her legs over the bed, being careful not to twist too far, and attempted to get out of bed with a slight lift. Her legs wobbled underneath her. She took hold of the bed to try and gain some control, but she was still heavily sedated. The doctor sprinted over to her side and quickly took her over her shoulders.

"Careful now," she said softly, "lean against the bed here, and I'll get you a wheelchair. I can tell you're anxious to get moving, but we had to give you a lot of sedatives. You took a hard hit against the side of the control panel."

She shuffled quickly to the far side of the med bay and went into a small supply closet, coming back out with a wheelchair in tow.

"Here you go!" She said in a chipper tone, "this should help get you around easy enough. If you end up needing further care, just come by and see me."

"Thanks, and what was your name again?"

"Doctor Ava Shint." She said matter-of-factly.

"Thanks, Doctor Shint. I'll let you know if there's anything else I need."

"Have a lovely day, miss Moon." The small woman began to shuffle across the med bay once again, monitoring the other patients one by one.

Zaz fiddled with the wheelchair for a few minutes until she got the hang of the controls and guided herself down the corridors toward the conference room. She was curious about who saved the entire fleet and was excited to learn what Jolene had to tell her. Jolene's thick accent came echoing from the conference room, followed by another voice that Zaz didn't recognize. It didn't sound like any of the other officers aboard the ship, at least not that she recalled. She entered the room to find Jolene sitting at the far end of the conference table, and directly to her right was standing a tall, built, figure.

When he noticed Zaz enter, he stood at attention and gave a slight bow. "Ah, miss Zaiza Moon I presume? I'm Jericho Davis, captain of the Atina fleet. It's a pleasure to meet your acquaintance."

"Uh, sure, nice to meet you too, Jericho. Are you the one that rescued us back there?"

"He sure as shit is, honey! Him and his boys were out here doin' their own scoutin' mission and caught wind of our distress signal. He flew on over and helped us out!" Jolene slapped Jericho on the back heartily, staggering him.

He straightened himself back out and addressed them both, "Well ladies, it was my pleasure to assist you in your time of need, and it's by pure chance that we're looking for the exact same person. Zavon Dash has been eluding our forces for some time now, but we've been narrowing in on him. We traced him back here to Evex after he took out a squadron of ours a few parsecs out from Grectum."

"What were you doing out by Grectum? Isn't that just a research moon?" Zaz asked.

"That's exactly correct, but we believe he's searching out advanced technology, so his appearance near there is not that odd. I'm sure you're all aware that Grellians have been salvaging Helix tech for years since Evex was destroyed. As the planetside tech became less abundant, they began stealing it off deliveries. More recently, however, they have been hijacking targeted traders because of more valuable machinery."

"Wait, that's how he knew about my work with Garreth! He must have found out that I was delivering the nanites and targeted my ship. Oh no..." Zaz suddenly felt hot, and her face turned white.

Jolene stood up and started toward her. "What is it, darlin'?"

"I took a delivery to Taric just before they dropped me off on Spada. He's got tons of weapons at the junkyard, and they probably tracked me down there." Her heart began racing, and she was feeling lightheaded.

"Alright now, calm down, honey. Jericho hit the toggle on the wall there and hand me a compress." She hustled over to Zaz, and Jericho tossed her the compress. She slapped the bag against the table to activate the chemicals inside and pressed it against the back of Zaz's neck. "We'll take care of it, but we came out here for another reason. You need to get those nanites for Garreth."

Zaz snapped out of her daze and refocused, "You're right. I need to find my ship, and I'm sure it's out there somewhere."

"Well, then I think I have some good news for you." Jericho pulled a datapad from his pocket and handed it to Zaz. "We found a large facility where the Grellians were storing many of the ships they stole. We haven't gotten down to check it out ourselves, but we certainly wouldn't mind. Do you have your ship's serial number handy?"

Zaz scrunched her face together and shook her head, "No, I'll be going with you."

"There's no way in hell you're goin' down there, Zaz. You've got a damned concussion and a set of broken ribs!" Jolene said firmly.

"Jolene, I'll be fine. First, I need to get to my ship and make sure they didn't find the nanites. Then I need to get back to Trexidia and make sure that Taric is okay."

"What about Garreth?"

"I'll tell him to expect another late delivery...."

| 10 |

A Dead Planet

Within an hour, Zaz found herself suited up and on the surface of Evex with a small team of soldiers led by Jericho. The planet was barren of any life, and gusts of sand blew relentlessly. Large slabs of rock jutted from the ground sporadically. Some looked like they were caused by explosions, others from something impossible to imagine. Across the landscape, Zaz could see numerous mining facilities, but all of them as lifeless as everything else on the planet.

The soldiers walked cautiously, checking for hidden enemies anywhere they could think of. Jericho, however, walked with the confidence that if he were to even be considered a target to shoot, they would die before they could pull the trigger. He was convinced his soldiers were the best out there, even better than that of P.A.R.O.L.E's, and he trusted them with his life entirely. Approaching the cavern expected to hold the stolen ships, the team stopped and allowed Jericho and Zaz to go ahead.

He turned to Zaz, "Well, this is it. We just need to find the entrance."

"Isn't that it right there?" She said, pointing at the maw of the cave.

He laughed, "Unfortunately, it's never quite that simple. Grellians may be stupid, but Zavon isn't. We've uncovered a few of his hidden bases, and it seems he's had them install hydraulic landing bays. It works out in their favor here on Evex. The sand pretty much covers them up within a few minutes." He pointed up the mountain. "We need to get up there and find the manual override. From there, we can lower ourselves down and hopefully find your ship."

Zaz peered up at the cliffside, feeling more exhausted the further her eyes climbed. "Well, we better get going then."

Jericho and Zaz climbed the jagged mountainside, scanning the surface for any sign of a control panel. The higher they climbed, the more narrow the mountain became, forcing them to traverse the worn cliffsides. The wind was relentless and growing in strength, buffeting their helmets with sand and now small chunks of rock. A big gust staggered Zaz forcing her to crouch down and brace herself against the cliffside. Jericho looked back at her and put his hand out. Grabbing hold of him, she pulled herself back up, and they worked their way to an outcropping that looked promising. Once they reached the clearing, Jericho started searching for a sign that the override was nearby. Zaz felt weak and decided to sit on the ledge taking in the view. She saw a small wire sticking out of the rocks, peering over the ridge. Following the trail, she noticed it ran up the wall of the mountain directly beneath her.

She looked back at Jericho, who was a good fifty yards away now, "Hey, I think I found something..." he didn't respond back or even look in her direction, "these comms are worthless. Do I really have to be right next to you to hear me?" Jericho continued his search, still oblivious to her call. "Screw it, I'll just do it myself."

Zaz scooted closer to the edge and started to descend to the minor cliffside. It was lower than she thought it would be, but she managed to get down to it without hurting herself. She found the wire again and started to pull it out from under the dust and rock that covered it. Tracing its path, she found a pile of stacked stones that were haphazardly thrown together. Tossing them aside, she found the control panel. She tried pulling the box open, but it was sealed shut. Pulling a hammer from her backpack, she broke open the box and found the override. Zaz flipped the toggle and looked out where the soldiers were waiting. The sand started shifting and revealed two massive hangar doors that swallowed the earth sitting on top of them. The guards looked up and waved at Zaz, who returned the acknowledgment.

Jericho's voice finally started to crackle into her headset, "Hey, you found it! Just in time too, the wind is really starting to get rough up here."

"Yeah, help me up from down here, and we'll get going."

Jericho obliged and tossed a rope down to her. Zaz tied it around her waist and pulled herself back up the ledge. Once she was back on the outcrop, Zaz took one last look at the desolate landscape of the planet. Looking to the east, she noticed a massive wall of sand heading in their direction.

"Holy shit, Jericho. Did you see that sand storm over there?"

"Yeah, we need to move if we're going to get off this mountain before that arrives. We don't want to end up in that mess."

The two started their descent and moved quickly, allowing their balance to set their pace, but the storm moved faster. Only minutes from the bottom of the mountain, the two were suddenly engulfed in the hulking squall. Jericho grabbed Zaz by the arm and quickly pulled her behind a boulder, shielding them from the wind. They covered their heads,blasts of gravel battering their suits. Zaz looked up for just a moment, only to be met with a rock smashing into her helmet and cracking the face shield.

"Jericho, we have a problem!" Zaz yelled, trying to speak over the loud winds.

"Yeah, this storm is insane! We just need to wait it out, and then we can meet up with the others."

"Not that," she said as her helmet began signaling alarms, "my helmet's busted. I'm going to start losing oxygen."

"Shit."

"Yeah, I've been saying that a lot lately...."

"I've got some duct tape in my bag. Let me see if I can get it. Do what you can to slow the leak."

The winds began picking up, blowing more debris down from the mountain top. Zaz held her hand to the crack in the helmet to try and stop the oxygen loss, but the strong gusts kept pushing it away. Jericho leaned into the boulder and loosened his bag from his back. Slipping his right arm out, he slung the bag around, but the wind caught hold of it and ripped it from his arm. It wedged itself between two rocks not far from where they were.

He groaned, "Well, isn't that just typical. Sit tight. I'll be back."

Zaz grabbed his arm tight and pulled him back toward her, "No, you sit tight. I don't need a valiant hero. I got myself into this mess, and I'll get myself out of it."

"Are you nuts? You're too weak to go out there yourself. You'll literally get blown away."

"Look, I'm tired of everyone else saving the day. Thanks for taking me out here to get my ship. If I die trying to get it, then that's on me."

She stood up and staggered immediately from a large gust of wind. Catching her balance, she started toward the pile of rocks, her helmet's alarms erupting a slew of new warnings. Zaz dismissed the notifications and continued forward. Rocks began hitting her from behind, but she kept her focus, ignoring the painful welts they were making. The oxygen meter on her helmet was depleting quickly and reached ten percent. Nine. Eight. Every second began to feel like her last. Getting the bag, she started rummaging through it. Whatever wasn't useful she tossed out, and the wind carried it miles away. Her monitor read three percent just as she came across the tape. She broke a piece off and slapped it over the crack. The leak seemed to stop, but the monitor dropped to two percent as soon as she took the first breath of relief. Panic was setting in. She felt all over the helmet, trying to find another leak. The monitor was at one percent now. Everywhere she could think of, she found no break or crack of any kind. Zero percent. A hand took the tape from her own, and she felt it grab hold of her oxygen tubes behind her.

"Oxygen levels are returning to normal." The helmet's echoed.

"Would you stop the whole hard-ass routine? You aren't stopping anyone if you're dead!" He let go of the oxygen tube and hunkered down behind the rock pile with her.

"I'm sorry," she said with heavy breaths, "I've just been... I don't know. I feel like I've just been riding everyone's coat-tails because of a mess I got myself into. It's like I have no control over my own destiny, and I just want that back."

"Look, you will, but you can't be reckless, or you'll end up dead. If the readings were right, your ship is right down there. We just need to make it through this storm, and you'll be in the pilot seat of your own destiny again."

"Thanks." Her voice resonated with the sound of embarrassment.

Jericho nudged her with his elbow and gave her a supportive look. The winds continued to barrel through for another half hour before they began to let up. The dust settled, and the valley below became visible again. The soldiers still stood, resolute and unmoving from their positions. Zaz and Jericho made their way back down the mountainside and to the open hatch.

"No detection of any life forms below, Sir." One of the stiff soldiers reported.

"Thank you, Lieutenant. Let's get some rope down there and rappel in. Remember, if you find anything of use, let's grab it. Otherwise, inventory what's down there, and we'll report it to P.A.R.O.L.E."

"You work for P.A.R.O.L.E.?" Zaz said with a quizzical look.

"We're one of their contract groups, yes. We've been working with them for years, but we're not an official branch. They don't care to come out this far from the inner planets and leave the outer rim to groups like us. We get paid well and get to keep anything that we want. It's a nice gig, overall. The only annoying part of the job is when Helix gets involved. Their androids try to flag everything as their tech, resulting in hours of paperwork and calls to their support staff."

"Oh, trust me, I know. Most of us traders have resorted to blasting them whenever we see them now. Trying to convince them it's not stolen isn't worth the wasted time, and when it is stolen, it's worth a whole lot more." She grinned, "Honestly, I'd say ninety percent of the traders out here are flagged as hostile."

Another soldier walked up to Zaz and handed her a zip line. She clipped it near her waist and walked to the edge of the hatch. The team went down into the hangar, and it became increasingly dark. After a few hundred yards, they fell into total darkness. The lights on their helmets activated, illuminating their faces and projecting light out into the unlit storage. Ships were everywhere. At least a thousand by Zaz's estimate. Some intact, others in pieces. When their feet touched the ground, they all unhooked themselves and started to patrol the area. Tankers, cruisers, escort vessels, ships of all types scattered the massive room.

Zaz surveyed the cavernous space, "Wow, I never thought Grellians could be capable of something like this."

Jericho came up beside her, "Yeah, it's pretty crazy, but

I guess with the right person leading them, they can do just about anything." He looked at the display in his helmet and sent the view over to Zaz. "According to this, your ship should be a few kilometers south of here."

"Then let's get going. Fingers crossed it's still in one piece."

They continued walking down the deep cavern with their footsteps echoing throughout. Zaz would occasionally see a ship or two that looked recognizable. Her mind started to process some of the stories she heard about different traders whose ships went missing or who went missing themselves. She wondered how long this had been going on. She hoped that some of the vessels would get returned to their owners, but she knew most of them wouldn't. Finally, they started to come across ships with less dust covering them. Looking at the monitor, she saw that her craft should be nearby.

Spotting a double-decker shuttle, Zaz tapped on Jericho's shoulder, "I'm going to climb up on that shuttle and see if I can't get a better look. They really packed these ships in here."

Jericho nodded, "Sounds good. I'm going to check a few of these ships since they might have some newer stuff inside that we can use."

The large, metallic purple ship had *Avante's Dream* painted across the side. It was a lovely ship meant for transporting large groups of people. Climbing up, Zaz peered in the window and saw the inside ransacked. A hint of dread began to seep into her mind wondering if her ship met a similar fate. Once she reached the top, she scanned the area, trying to spot *The Avius* amongst the hundreds of other ships in this quadrant of the hangar. About a hundred yards to her left, she spotted it. The emerald green paint job still shined as clean as the day she had it painted. On top, she saw the small Rovo bot, damaged from the hook that shot into it only a few days earlier. She crawled back down to the ground level and started to hoof it toward her ship.

What started as a jog became a sprint, followed by a full-on run. Zaz missed her ship. She missed the comfort of her own pilot seat, the cluttered mess of the cockpit, and her bed. She missed everything about it, and she was finally going to get it back. Her ribs started to ache as she ran past the rows of derelict ships. She didn't care and pushed past the pain. Finally, Zaz rounded what she knew was the last turn she would need to make, and right in front of her sat *The Avius.* It was still just as she had last seen it. Surprisingly, the Grellians had not torn it up or crashed it from poor piloting skills. She ran up to the loading bay door and keyed in her access code. The hydraulics hissed as they released the platform lowering it down so she could enter. She held her breath. The last thing she saw was them tearing chunks of her ship out to find Garreth's nanites, and who knew what they did to it afterward. The door was finally open.

She stepped inside and saw a few panels torn off of the storage bay walls, but nothing that couldn't be repaired. Stepping inside the main corridor, everything was still intact except for the hidden compartment she was smuggling the nanites and extra credits in. Overall, everything looked fine. Streaks of slime lined the walls of the small corridor. Zaz knew the Grellian in charge of flying must have been one of the bigger ones that could barely fit.

"Oh no," She grimaced, "I bet my seat is going to be covered in that crap."

She reached the cockpit and stood outside the closed door. Keying in the access code, the door slid open and revealed the mess she called home. She felt a sudden relief, as though just seeing this room meant everything was going to be okay. The floor was covered in trade log paperwork and the trinkets that generally sat on the console. Just as she imagined, the seat itself was covered in the same slime that coated the corridor outside. With a heavy sigh, she dug around for a towel and wiped it clean. Finally, she plopped down into her seat and stroked the armrests with a spark of joy. She flipped the console on, and the ship came back to life. The monitors began their bootup sequence, and the jets started their startup sequence.

Jericho's voice came through the helmet's comm, "Hey is that you, Zaz? Did you find her?"

"Roger that Jericho, The Avius in perfect condition! Well... close enough to perfect!" Let's get the hell out of here and find that rat bastard!"

"Sounds like a winner! If you don't mind giving us a lift out of here, we'll board our own ship and escort yourself and Jolene to Trexidia and see if we can't find and arrest Zavon."

"It would be my absolute pleasure." She said with a fierce determination now in her voice.

Grabbing the controls in her hands with a firm grip, she powered on the thrusters and lifted the ship off the ground. The dust that covered the surrounding vessels swirled around the cavern. The ship was running smooth, and the grin on Zaz's face grew more prominent with every movement the ship made. Seeing Jericho, Zaz piloted the ship down into the clearing for him to board.

"Wow, this is a pretty nice ship minus the slime on the walls."

"Yeah, well, if you don't mind, there are some work rags in the cabinet back there. So make yourself useful for once." She said, laughing.

Zaz picked up the rest of the team along with the supplies they deemed valuable and took them back to the surface of the planet. Once they were aboard their own ship, she pointed *The Avius* toward the sky and gave the thrusters full power. The ship leaped forward, leaving a crater in the sand as it rocketed toward space and toward Zaz's next destination.

| 11 |

Revelations and Reckonings

The engineers aboard Jolene's transport were happy to help Zaz get her ship cleaned up and back to normal. Jolene instructed them to ensure everything was fixed up, and a new Rovo unit was installed. Zaz said she would happily pay for the repairs, but Jolene wouldn't take it. It was amazing to have such a great friend, someone who would do anything for her, and she was determined to one day pay her back for everything Jolene had done for her in the last few days.

Jericho and the Atina fleet did as he said they would and created an escort toward Trexidia. However, it was going to be a long trip due to Texidia's rotation around the sun. It moved much faster than other outer rim planets and was already leagues away from where it was when Zaz was last there. This meant that if Zavon was heading for Trexidia, he would be there days before Zaz arrived. With what she saw on Evex, she shuddered to think of what he would be capable of on a living planet with usable tech. She attempted to contact Taric, but there was no connection available. A pit in her stomach grew as she considered the possibilities of what that meant. She could only hope that he was able to defend himself or hide from the danger that was surrounding his home.

She had been dreading the following call since she lost her ship, and that was to let Garreth know she had lost the nanites. She considered not making the call at all, but Jolene urged her to let him know in case he might be able to help. She argued that he may be able to tell Zaz what she really lost. Begrudgingly she agreed and called him from the command center. Standing in front of the monitor, the pit in her stomach started to harden. She pulled up the directory on screen and dialed in his communications code. The speakers echoed its standard dial tone and connected.

"Hello, this is Garreth; with whom am I speaking?"

Zaz hesitated and swallowed the rock in her throat, "Hey Garreth, it's Zaz."

His tone was excited and chipper, "Ah! So good to hear from you! I suspect you should be arriving soon with the nanites, correct?"

"Uhm, well, not exactly. You see, there's been a complication...."

She continued to tell Garreth all the events leading up to where they were now. The further she got into the story, the more she used sarcasm to push down her nervousness. It was a coping mechanism she had long been accustomed to using, and she hoped it would help relieve the anger Garreth might be feeling.

"And so you see, I didn't lose them so much as they were forcibly removed from my possession."

"Zaiza, I entrusted you with these deliveries because you assured me nothing would happen to them while in your hands. I've overlooked the late arrivals because they arrived in perfect condition, but this is highly concerning. The Tycho-sheen nanites have the immense ability to regenerate organic tissue. They're a medical advancement like we have never seen before." Garreth said matter-of-factly.

"Yeah, no, I totally understand, and I'm fully working on getting them back...."

"Well, I hope you can. It sounds like this Zavon person is quite intelligent, and he's likely done his research on my work. He targeted you for a reason, and I'm concerned about what he has planned for my technology."

"It just doesn't make sense why he would want the nanites, though."

"As I said, they have restorative properties that have not been fully tested. Perhaps he is looking for a way to heal his wounded quicker. From the sound of it, he has been amassing an army. My fear is that he plans to bring war to the inner planets. Perhaps he is tired of living on the outskirts, and the Grellians are as well."

"Well, we've got the Atina fleet with us, so hopefully, we can deter that from happening. I'll get the nanites back, Garreth. I promise you I will."

Garreth sighed, "I'm confident you will, and I thank you for bringing this to my attention."

"Of course." Zaz terminated the connection and plopped into a nearby chair.

With potential war now on the table, Zaz began considering what that could look like. In her encounter with Zavon's ship, she recalled the Grellians were more coordinated than she first considered. Grellians were typically disorganized and hardly stood still long enough to take direction. Why didn't she notice that before? Her mind tried to recall her meeting with the two goons at the cantina. They seemed normal enough. One giant burly oaf, and a skinny ratlike chatterbox, both of who could barely compose themselves. Nothing like the Grellians on Zavon's ship. Something was missing, but she just couldn't pin it down.

She pushed the chair back and lifted herself out. "Enough sitting around. I need to clear my head." Then, striding out of the command center, she went down to her ship.

As she reached the docking bay, she was greeted by one of the engineers. "Hello, Ms. Moon. We've cleaned up your ship and have installed a new Rovo unit. Everything seems to be running smoothly."

"That's great! Tell Jolene I appreciate all of this, and thanks to your team."

"Of course, ma'am. Also, we've taken the courtesy to update your thruster controls with a T183 processor. It'll give you a little more kick when you're planetside instead of having to take it low and steady."

"Sick! Is that what you use here?"

"To an extent, yes. Since *Jolene's Dream* is such a large ship, we use a T1000, but it gives us great control when you're in a gravitational zone. That's how we can outmaneuver the Helix androids so easily." He motioned toward a ship draped over with a large cloth, "Oh, and as an extra thank you from the crew, we decided your ship needed a bit of a paint job while we were at it."

They walked toward the ship, and the surrounding engineers pulled the cloth off of the ship, revealing the now fire-red *Avius.* Zaz's eyes grew wide, accompanied by a smile from ear to ear. Finally, her eyes began to water, and happiness overcame her. She hugged the engineer so tight he let out a slight cough. "It's wonderful! Thank you so much, seriously...."

"It was the least we could do after you took control of the guns and saved our hides. If it wasn't for you pulling Pete out of that gunner seat and shooting down the Z30s, we would have taken on more damage than we did. We're not sure we would have made it out alive." He put a hand out and firmly shook Zaz's, "Plus, your ship looked a little worn. Jolene and the whole crew think you deserve better than that. Especially after everything you've been going through. Why don't you look inside and take it for a spin? Tell us how we did."

Her hand brushed the fresh paint job as she walked the ship's perimeter. The red paint was accented with black striping that circled around the thrusters. It was the best the ship had ever looked. Stepping inside the loading bay, she made her way toward the cockpit. The corridor recently covered in slime had been cleaned and polished, along with new lighting installed along the walkways. When Zaz reached her destination, she first noticed the floor, now devoid of all the random paperwork and trinkets. Instead, everything in the room was sparkling clean and sparkled with chrome knobs. It was like she had just purchased a new ship off the assembly line.

She sat down in the pilot's seat. Its cushioning, still the original just scrubbed clean, offered a familiar comfort that reminded her it was still her ship. Her hands gripped the thruster controls, and the control panel came to life. Pressing the power button on the side of one control, she heard the thrusters wail to life. In front of her, she saw the bay doors opening, inviting her to open space. Her jaw was set in a determined look as a smirk cut across her face. An engineer signaled the all-clear, and she pulled back on the controls. The ship ripped through the landing bay and out into the black expanse before her. The ship was leaps and bounds better than ever, and Zaz felt the best she had in weeks. Flying at max speed, cutting sharp turns, and having the joy ride of her life, she couldn't help but laugh out loud and get excited for the fight that was soon to come.

| 12 |

Battlegrounds of the Cosmos

Approximately three days later, the fleet was finally falling upon Trexidian space. Upon approaching the junkyard planet, the team could see thousands of ships surrounding it. There was no denying that it was Zavon's army. Jericho had reached out to P.A.R.O.L.E and requested backup and was informed that they would attempt to send assistance as quickly as possible. This was far beyond anything they had anticipated. Questions on how they stayed out of sight for so long began circulating across communications. The following steps of the Atina fleet demanded that everyone pull back and wait for the arrival of P.A.R.O.L.E's team and to prepare for the impending battle.

"So we're just supposed to sit here while they occupy Trexidia? What about Taric? Why can't we punch a line through and get planetside?" Zaz had been pacing back and forth in the command center, anxious and ready to fight.

Jericho's voice came over the comm link, "We're outnumbered to an insane degree. It would be suicide to even attempt it. However, P.A.R.O.L.E is on their way with a significant backup fleet, and then we can order them to stand down."

"Ugh, fine. I'm just bored out of my mind and want to get this over with. I'm tired of standing around."

"We all are, darlin'," Jolene said with a slight grin, "but we'll be kicking ass in no time once we have some more firepower. I might have a lot of firepower here, but you saw how quickly we got flooded by them Z30s. This is a lot more than that."

Zaz nodded, "Yeah, I know. So, where should we wait? I feel like floating around here isn't the best place."

"We're far enough out that they shouldn't be able to detect us, but it wouldn't be bad to fall back a bit more in case they decide to start perimeter scans," Jericho said. "There's an asteroid field a few clicks out that we can sit in while we wait.

"Sounds like a plan; we'll fall back there and wait with ya." Jolene agreed.

Upon settling into the asteroid field, the teams began preparing themselves for battle. Jolene's crew ran diagnostics on the various blasters throughout the ship and prepped the few combat cruisers they had on board. Zaz sat in her cruiser, putting her bobbles back on her control panel. Then, with the final piece set in place with a glob of sticky putty, she kicked her feet up on the dashboard and dozed off as she waited for the excitement to happen.

After a few hours, Zaz was woken up by a ping coming

through the comms. She sat up, groggy after finally getting some good sleep, and tied her ship into the feed. A report began feeding throughout the ship's communication relay with an autonomous tone. "Attention, this is the Helix Industries Tracker fleet 11031. You are in violation of Helix Industries trade authorization article 1729 section B, the unlawful trading of Helix technology, and article 4173 section A, the destruction or dismantling of Helix Industries Tracker units. By the sanctions vested in Helix Industries by the Outer Rim Policing Alliance, you, and all current associates, have been deemed a criminal nuisance and are hereby subject to termination."

Zaz rubbed her eyes and squinted at the monitor, "Huh?" Then, she leaned forward and pressed the relay to play back the message.

"Attention, this is the Helix Industries Tracker fleet 11031. You are in violation of Helix Industries trade authorization article 1729 section B, the unlawful trading of Helix technology, and article 4173 section A, the destruction or dismantling of Helix Industries Tracker units. By the sanctions vested in Helix Industries by the Outer Rim Policing Alliance, you, and all current associates, have been deemed a criminal nuisance and are hereby subject to termination." The android said again.

The words processed in her mind for the second time, followed by the angry voice of Jolene coming through the comm relay, "God damn it! I thought I lost these shitheads back at Spada. Everyone to your stations, and get ready for a fight!" Sirens started to sound across the loading bay, and the engineers began to scramble to get to a secure location.

Throwing her feet off the dashboard, Zaz grabbed her comm device and called out to Jolene, "I thought Helix didn't come out this far!"

"Looks like they're expandin' their reach, darlin'."

Zaz reached across the dash and powered on her ship's thrusters. The engine's hum and the excitement of a dog fight sent goosebumps down her body. The other pilots fell in line, one by one zipping out of the docking station. She followed suit and pulled her ship into position. With the departure of the leading ship, Zaz punched her thrusters and rocketed into the blackness of space.

The surrounding asteroids littered the area. From her viewport, Zaz could see the various ships of the Atina fleet accompanied by Jolene's crew. The scanners began to ping the Tracker fleet. At first, it was only a few dots indicating the incoming threat. Easy enough to eliminate without causing a stir, Zaz thought. Still, after a few seconds, a wave of red washed over the screen in their direction.

"Oh, fuck..."

"Oh, fuck is right," Jericho's voice came over the comm system.

Staring in the direction of the incoming swarm, everyone could see the intimidating size of the fleet. Zaz tried to count them, but it was an impossible task. She estimated about four to five thousand at least. Her palms began to sweat as she gripped the controls of her ship tighter. Looking to her left, she could see Jericho's ship. He was staring at the fleet as well, unmoving. She wondered how he was feeling, but deep down, she knew he was just as scared as she was. They weren't just outnumbered, but their sheer number would signal Zavon's army as well.

"First one to a hundred buys the first round," she said jokingly, trying to break the silence.

Jericho chuckled, "Tell you what, you take down two hundred, and I'll buy drinks for everyone here."

"You heard 'em folks, drinks are on Jericho after this is all over! My money's on Zaz." Jolene's cheerful voice gave Zaz a reassuring resilience.

"Well, enough waiting around for them." Zaz pulled back on her thrusters and launched toward the oncoming fleet. "Let's take these fuckers down!"

The momentum pushed her back in her seat. She reached out and smacked her lucky bobblehead, a purple Nargutz beast from Edic. Then, leading the pack, Zaz made right for the Trackers. Entering their proximity, she flipped the charging switch for the ion cannon.

One of the Trackers came across the comm system, "Incoming vessel, identify yourself. You are approaching the Helix Tracker Fleet…."

"Yeah, yeah, yeah, eat shit." She cut in and pulled the trigger. A bright yellow ball released from the cannon landed directly in front of the oncoming Tracker fleet. It erupted in a brilliant light that only lasted a second. Scrap metal of fifty-plus ships littered the area.

"You have attacked a Helix Industries fleet. Prepare to be pursued." A new Tracker voice stated firmly.

Zaz rolled her ship back and throttled toward the asteroid field. The remaining Tracker ships began to separate and move into attack positions. Red blasts began firing toward

Zaz and the others around her. Members of the Atina fleet and Jolene's crew followed suit, opening fire, and lighting up the once dark section of space. Tracker ships blew to pieces one after the other as the hail of blaster fire fell upon them.

Breaking away from the barrage, a group of Tracker ships followed Zaz into the asteroid field. Zipping through the rocky obstacle course, she attempted to lose as many as possible. A hard bank around one asteroid followed by a steep dive underneath another. The Trackers were highly skilled at calculating trajectories around the debris and closed in on her quickly. She needed a quick escape route to shake them.

Her radar began to sound off an alert siren that blared through her audio system, "ENEMY PURSUIT DETECTED. FORTY-FIVE SHIPS IDENTIFIED AND COUNTING. COVER RECOMMENDED." Zaz smacked the radar attempting to silence it. Two blasts went off on either side of her ship, activating the radar again, "INCOMING MISSILES DETECTED."

"Ah, gee ya think?" she yelled out frustratedly.

Zaz skimmed her ship as close to the asteroids as she could without risking one floating into her. Ahead she saw a pair of large asteroids beginning to collide. It was a risky play to try and squeeze between them, but the hairier the situation, the more determined she was to make it happen. Slamming her throttle forward, the ship lurched back before erupting a mass of fuel into the engines. It roared to life and rocketed toward the ever-shrinking space between the rocks. The Trackers followed suit and ignited their own machines.

"WARNING INCOMING COLLISION WITH AST-" Zaz cut the alarm off before it could finish.

"Enough with the warnings!" She cried out over the blaring sirens. "I've heard enough of them over the last few days. Reroute all power to the engines!"

"ORDER ACKNOWLEDGED."

The lights inside the cabin went dark except for the few indicators glowing on the control panel. The sirens and alarms stopped, and the entire ship became eerily quiet except for the engines behind her. With a jerk, the ship accelerated to a speed it wasn't built for. The cabin began to fill with the sound of rattling junk that wasn't bolted down.

Through the viewport of The Avius, Zaz could see the space between her and the massive rocks growing smaller and smaller. A bead of sweat began rolling down her forehead as she wondered if she had made the right decision. She gripped the controls of the ship tight, her knuckles turning white. Behind her, ships were being crushed. Explosions were flooding through the small space catching up to her faster than the Trackers could. The force of the engines matched with the blasts engulfing the vessel and began rattling the ship. Pieces of metal plating began falling off the interior from the bolts shaking loose, and flight logs began littering the floor again. Her nerves started to get the best of her.

With only inches of space left, Zaz saw the end of the asteroids just on the horizon. She pushed the throttle, but it couldn't move any further. The asteroids continued to collapse on one another, and she could hear the back of the ship begin to scrape across them. Zaz closed her eyes, expecting to listen to the explosion of her own engines. Instead, the scraping sound stopped, and all that was left was the sound of the engines continuing to rage forward. She opened her eyes instead to an incoming asteroid. She pulled up on the controls and dodged around it. Circling back, she noticed none of the Trackers made it through.

"Well, by my count, that's about a hundred and twenty for me." She laughed into her commlink.

"A hundred and eight, to be exact." Jericho fired back.

Jolene's voice cut through on the comm, "Folks, hate to break up the fun, but it looks like our Grellian friends noticed our scuffle. They're movin' in on us quick."

"Roger that, Jolene," said Jericho. "We can maneuver our team to intercept, but it will be rough. Might lose a couple in the exchange."

"Don't worry about it, darlin'. I'll take care of the Grellians. You finish off these damned Trackers." She replied.

"I'll be there to back you up soon, just have to navigate back out of the asteroid field." Zaz turned her ship back toward the ensuing dog fight and cranked the throttle back down again. Then, the remaining lights on her console suddenly went dark with a flicker, and the engines cut out. "Ah, shit..."

"SYSTEM REBOOT INITIATED. POWER CYCLING IS REQUIRED. ESTIMATED TIME FOR REIGNITION...30 MINUTES."

Zaz cupped her face in her hands. "Are you serious right now..." she muffled.

As the ship entered its power cycling phase, Zaz was left floating amongst the asteroids. From her viewport, she could see the light show of the battle in the distance. Jolene's ship was large enough to easily see it adjust its direction and head toward Trexidia and the incoming Grellian fleet. Unable to help and stranded in place, she felt miserable and helpless once again.

| 13 |

Stranded Again

The reboot sequence felt like an eternity to Zaz. Her position provided a perfect view of the ensuing battle, however. The Atina fleet was incredibly skilled, she thought to herself. She was happy they were on her side. Hundreds of exploding Tracker ships lit up the scene before her, and the itch to join them continued to fester. With the power out, the silence within the ship grew increasingly louder until she couldn't stand it any longer. She tapped her fingers on the command console with irritation just to break the silence and let out a grumble of frustration.

"Please. Just hurry up and reboot...."

The sound of Zaz's stomach broke the silence. With the recent excitement of everything, she realized she had forgotten to eat. Kicking the piles of logs at her feet, Zaz jerked herself up from the pilot seat. Her face twinged in pain, and she grabbed her ribs. They were still sore but seemed to at least be getting better. She grabbed her headlamp hanging from the console and made her way out of the cockpit.

She walked into the ship's cabin and made her way to the kitchen. The entire ship was a mess. Metal panels and bolts covered the floors exposing the wiring throughout the ship. Supplies were scattered around, and drawers hung open, but no food was in sight.

The counter where Zaz had her secret storage compartment and once held Garreth's nanites looked like a complete disaster. She let out a heavy sigh and started to clean up the mess. Stacking empty containers back in the cabinets and closing the open drawers, she came across one drawer that seemed jammed. Then, with a swift kick, she felt the drawer come loose, followed by a faint clinking sound of something falling into the drawer below.

Pulling open the bottom drawer revealed a small metal vial rolling toward Zaz. Her eyes widened with the realization that it was one of the nanite vials.

"No. Fucking. Way..."

Her hand darted toward the vial and snatched it out of the drawer. She spun it around with her fingers, analyzing every detail of it. The vial turned in her hand to reveal the small window on the side, and she noticed a fresh crack. Flooding out of the break were tiny, green nanites. Her eyes followed the path the vial had just taken across her hand, and she noticed the small machines making their way along her arm and toward her ribcage.

A rush of panic washed over her body in fear of losing the few nanites she had salvaged, followed by a sudden wave of relief. She could feel the nanites repairing the tiny fractures in her ribs. At the same time, she felt the bandaging that was wrapped around her start fusing to her skin.

"Whoa, that's not OK." She lurched out in a mixture of surprise and disgust.

She threw her shirt off and grabbed a sharp piece of metal to cut the wrapping off. With a bit of a struggle, she managed to cut apart the bandage on one side and started pulling. The area where the nanites converged had become an odd amalgamate of skin and fabric. She tugged at the site, but it was no use. The two had become blended together.

"Well...I can't say this is the weirdest thing that's ever happened to me, but it's not my favorite...." Zaz groaned as she cut off the un-fused part of the bandage and put her shirt back on.

The lights in the cabin came on as she threw the remains of her wrap on the ground. While the feeling of her fused skin was odd, she appreciated the lack of pain in her ribs. The hunger that had spurred her to venture into the kitchen was gone.

She made her way back to the cockpit and flopped into her chair, ready to get back into action.

"Reconnect with the Atina fleet and Jolene." She commanded the computer.

"ORDER ACKNOWLEDGED. INCOMING TRANSMISSION FROM JOLENE."

"Hey, Darlin, where the hell are you at? We could use you...." Jolene cut off for a moment, "Incoming photon blast hold tight!" The sound of a large explosion followed by sirens filled the transmission. "We're going down, I repeat, we are going down! Prepare for an emergency landing on Trexidia."

"TRANSMISSION ENDED."

The wave of panic from earlier came back with a vengeance, and Zaz felt herself get cold and clammy. She grit her teeth and gripped the thruster controls with all her strength. It was her fault that Jolene was a part of this, and now it might be her fault that Jolene dies. She couldn't let that happen. She wouldn't let that happen. Zaz powered the controls back on and slammed the thrusters to full speed on a direct path to Trexidia.

| 14 |

Back to Trexidia

Dashing through the vast space between her and Trexidia, Zaz witnessed the still ensuing battle between the Atina and Tracker fleets that had now entwined themselves with Grellian fighters. The Trackers had precision coordination in their flight formations. Still, their poor programming did little to help their aim. The Grellians fought dirty, firing at any engaged units they could find and even suiciding into them. One after another, ships from all sides erupted in flames creating a display of fireworks and shrapnel.

Zaz routed her ship directly through the battle, adding to her earlier tally, lighting up every Tracker and Grellian in her path. Finally, she called out over the comm system, "Jericho, come in. What's the status of your crew?"

"Welcome back, Zaz. We've lost a few, but overall we're holding our own. The Grellians joining in was actually helpful." He replied.

"What's the status on Jolene and her crew?" She responded with a stern determination.

"Ship touched the planet side about five minutes ago. Got swarmed by some Grellian bombers that took out her shields. We can't peel away to get over there, though."

"What's the E.T.A. on P.A.R.O.L.E.?"

There was a pause before answering, "Not sure. I haven't heard from them since our last communication. They could still be hours out for all I know..."

Zaz keyed in on an unsuspecting Grellian frigate and took out its engines before rolling in and blowing up the command deck. "Guess we're on our own then. You keep your team alive. I'll handle Jolene."

"Zaz, we don't even know what the ground level looks like. It could be a suicide mission." Jericho said with a hint of concern in his voice.

"I know Trexidia well enough. Taric has plenty of places where I can take cover and survey the area. Then, all I have to do is find Jolene, and we can take one of the Grellian ships."

"Alright, if you say so."

"Trust me, it's gonna be the easiest thing I've ever done. Well, maybe the second easiest..." She lined her ship up behind a wave of Tracker ships and fired into them one after the other, "that's two hundred, by the way." She smirked and pivoted her ship back on course for Trexidia.

"Looks like drinks are on me then." He chuckled.

| 15 |

Uncovering the Truth

Within a few minutes, Zaz entered the atmosphere of Trexidia. While some Grellian patrols were hovering around the area, most had occupied themselves with chasing down Jolene's ship. In contrast, the rest were occupied with the Tracker brigade that broke away from the primary battle. That gave Zaz the cover she needed to slip through and down toward the planet.

The lime green atmosphere was particularly thick today. A chem storm was brewing which gave her rescue mission a tighter deadline. Sinking past the upper atmosphere, the view became clear. She scanned the landscape in search of the downed ship. Rolling hills of compacted trash painted the scenery along with the acidic rivers and lakes for which the planet was famous. About fifteen kilometers to her East, Zaz spotted the smoke of the crash. She set the ship on course and continued to scout the area.

After getting her bearings, she realized that only thirty

kilometers North of the crash site was Taric's mountain bunker. Getting closer to Jolene's ship, Zaz peered out toward the mountain and noticed a swarm of Grellian frigates and fighters littering the area. Looking closer, she noticed that there was a telescopic-looking structure at the mountain's peak that wasn't there before.

"I'll check that out after we get Jolene sorted." She said to herself.

Pulling up to the crash site, she noticed that the Grellian ships she expected to be swarming the wreck were nothing but scrap metal. Hovering above the downed ship, she saw a small crew of Jolene's outside flagging Zaz. She landed without hesitation and rushed out to meet the crew.

"Boy, are we happy to see you!" One of the crew members yelled out.

"Hey, where's Jolene? Is everyone OK?" Zaz said with a slight panic in her tone.

"Jolene is up in the command deck. Everyone's OK, just a few bumps and bruises from the initial crash. Once we landed, Jolene put all power into the shields, and it saved us from the suicide bombers."

Zaz looked around at all the rubble and scrap metal lying around the ship. She took a closer look at some of the larger pieces. In the same instant as picking it up, she dropped it and staggered backward in horror.

The crew member walked up and asked, "What is it? What's wrong?"

"The. They. Oh my god." Zaz held her hand to her mouth to repel a gag, "They're fused to the metal. They aren't just suicide pilots. They're part of the ship!"

She bolted into Jolene's ship and ran up to the command room, barging in. Jolene jumped back at the sudden intrusion and whirled her pistol toward Zaz before dropping it back in her holster and running up to give Zaz a massive hug.

"Oh, darlin', you've got no idea how good it is to see you!"

"It's good to see you too, Jolene, but I've got some bad news." Her voice trembled.

Jolene's face turned from joyful to severe, and she grabbed Zaz firmly by the shoulders, "Alright, hun, deep breath and tell me what's goin' on."

Zaz took a deep breath and continued, "Zavon, he's using the nanites that Gareth created to fuse the Grellians to the ships. The nanites can heal, but I don't think they're perfected. I found a few in my ship, and they fixed the fractures in my ribs but sewed my shirt into my skin a bit."

"Well, that just doesn't make any damn sense, Zaz. Why would he be fusin' the Grellians to their ships?"

"I...I don't know. Maybe he knows something we don't? Or maybe he's testing the limits of the nanites? I can't say, but he's also working on something big over at Taric's bunker. I couldn't get a good look at it, but I can't imagine it's good."

Jolene bit down on her lower lip with an inquisitive look, "Well, looks like you're gonna have to go find out then, darlin'."

Zaz shook her head in defiance, "What? No, I just came to get you out of here. We can leave the rest to P.A.R.O.L.E or something."

"We can handle ourselves while you check in on that," Jolene said with a firm authority that Zaz had only heard during their first encounter with the Grellians. "That horde of snot jockeys are still dumber than a box of scraps. The ones that followed us killed themselves in the bombardment, so we should be in the clear for a while. Our systems are self-repairing, so we have about half an hour before we're up and runnin' again. That's plenty of time to discover what's goin' on and circle back."

Zaz nodded and took a deep breath she had been holding in, "Right, OK."

"Don't forget to find Taric and ensure he's alright." She loosened her grip on Zaz's shoulders and flashed a solicit grin. "Go on now!"

Zaz spun on her heels and booked it out of Jolene's ship. Her thoughts overwhelmed her. One stupid decision had led to so many lives being at stake. A decision she made, and for what? A few extra credits? Tears flooded her eyes, and she tripped over a slab of debris falling into the viscera that was mud on this planet. A sob broke away from her, and she realized it was the most vulnerable she had ever felt. Her hand curled into a fist and punched the ground. Wiping the tears from her face, she picked herself up and grit her teeth. She boarded her ship and sat in the pilot's seat. She felt the tears attempting to come back, but she forced them down. Gripping the controls with her muddy hands, she engaged the ship and lifted it into a hover above Jolene's. She peered down at the few crew members working on the ship's exterior and then at the command window where Jolene was peering back from. They gave each other a knowing nod, and Zaz turned her attention toward the mountain bunker and took off.

| 16 |

Racing Against Time

Taking to the clouds as cover, Zaz piloted her ship slowly. She knew most radar systems wouldn't alert vehicles that moved at the standard P.A.R.O.L.E instituted "safe" speeds. Instead, her eyes were locked on the pale green vapor that covered her view, and her thoughts were honed on ending whatever Zavon had planned. Gripping the controls tighter, she sunk deeper into her seat.

The nav system pinged an alert as she approached the bunker. Skimming just below the clouds, Zaz saw the elaborate carbide steel gates of the hangar she flew into only a few short weeks ago. From the outside, everything looked normal except for the various junker ships parked carelessly around the exterior. There weren't even Grellians guarding them. She guided her ship in closer and noticed the lower section of the gates looked damaged.

"Scan the gates." She ordered her ship.

"GATE INTEGRITY COMPROMISED. SEVERE HEAT AND IMPACT DAMAGE."

She slammed her balled fist onto the armrest of her seat, "Damnit, so they did get in...."

She glanced up above the bunker and saw the same towering object she had noticed earlier. Up close, she realized it was a colossal monolith of scrap metal that came to a sharp peak. Broad trenches of what looked like wiring ran from the object's base to the top. Clearly, they were building some kind of gadget, but she wasn't sure what. She recalled seeing something similar when she was on Evex. They had been planning this all along, practicing on planets that no one would think twice about. Was Trexidia always the last stop? What did the nanites have to do with all of this? There were more questions than she had answers to, but maybe she could find them inside the bunker.

Spotting a small cave nearby, she maneuvered the ship inside and landed. The cave was ripe with the smell of toxic sludge seeping out of the soil above. The sound of construction could be heard everywhere, which told Zaz she would have to keep an eye to not get spotted. She held her hand up to her nose and made her way out. Peeking around the mouth of the cave, she saw there was a clear path leading up to the gates. She quickly dashed to the port and looked at the various outside ships. It was odd that none of them were guarded, but then she noticed the stomach-churning reality. On the nose of every ship, there was a guard. They were fused to the ship, suspended above the ground staring in whatever direction the ship faced. She paused as she noticed the eyes of one of them nearby caught her gaze. They looked at each other for a long time before the engines on the ship ignited. Her eyes widened. She didn't understand how that was possible, but it all became clear. The nanites didn't just fuse their skin to whatever they touched. It made them one and the same. The Grellians were the ships, and now one of the guards was literally taking off to alert the rest.

She reached to her hip, pulled out her pistol, and fired off a single skilled shot right into the head of the guard. The engines died, and the ship came to a quick touch down. Her head swiveled around, looking for any other ships facing her direction. None seemed to be alerted to her presence. Finally, with the gateway only a few feet away, she made a mad dash and found the break in the steel where Zavon and his crew forced their way in. She flung herself inside and immediately pressed up against the wall.

"Shit, that was close!" she whispered with quick breaths.

The sound of grunt work brought her focus back, and she slowly worked her way through the makeshift corridor cut out of the steel gates. Reaching the end of the passage, she saw a pile of crates and other junk scattered across the immediate space as though it had been blown out when this crater was made. Amongst the debris were the bodies of a few Trexidians that she recalled sorted through the Helix tech she brought in. She hoped that Taric hadn't shared a similar fate.

Looking back into the hangar, she noticed a handful of Grellians loading scrap metal and assorted tech into crates and hauling them toward a makeshift ramp leading up to the massive pillar above. A couple of guards walked around aimlessly with large electron rifles. Behind them was Taric's office, where she could access security cameras and hopefully find out where he was being held. She grabbed a piece of rubble from the ground and looked around for something to hit. A shelf of small scrap sat in a small corridor on the opposite side of the office. She chucked the hunk of debris, and it clanged against a basket of scrap, making a loud noise. The guards looked startled and began grunting and shoving one another as they tried to get the other to check out the sound.

"Idiots, just go," she sighed, rolling her eyes.

She picked up another piece of rubble and hit the basket a second time. Finally, after more pushing and shoving, they both conceded and began approaching the corridor with their rifles drawn. Once she had a clear path toward the office, she sprinted toward the office and ducked inside. Keeping low to the ground, she worked her way behind the counter where the safe resided and the door to Taric's personal office. The safe was still locked up, and Zaz noticed that the entire office generally seemed almost untouched. Ducking into the office, she closed the door and pulled down the blinds.

The surveillance system was in sleep mode. After pressing various buttons on the console, the backlit screens powered on and illuminated the room. Her eyes darted from screen to screen, scanning for any hint of Taric. Grellians were in almost every part of the facility, scavenging for whatever they could find. It was typical of their species to land on a planet and strip it of anything with a nominal value, but this was different. They were using everything on the structure above.

After a few more minutes of scanning and flipping through different views, Zaz spotted her reptilian friend locked in a makeshift cage. He looked bruised and beaten to within an inch of his life. His breaths were short and quick. In the top right corner was the location designation: UPPER DOCKING BAY, ZONE 3. An isometric layered map was displayed on the opposite wall of the monitors. The location was at the base of the structure they had built, which meant Zaz was going to get her hands dirty. She rested her palm on the butt of her pistol and walked toward the office door.

Looking through the blinds, she counted the number of targets immediately outside. Two guards, each with rifles and poor aim, and six workers, all near an accessible exit. The exits were cargo bays with steel doors that would drop closed when an alarm was activated but wouldn't open again. Her eyes darted around the room and locked in on a vent on the other end of the warehouse leading out to the upper docking bay. Looking down at the outside counter, she saw what she assumed was an emergency alarm. She figured it was used more by Taric to lock people in than keep people out, but that's exactly what she needed.

With a deep breath, she flung open the door and stepped back into the larger office, hand saddled on the hilt of the pistol Jolene gifted her. Reaching the counter, she pressed the button underneath it, and a thunderous alarm began to blare across the warehouse. Before the Grellians had time to react to the alarm, the bay doors slammed to the ground with an echoing thud. One of them was unlucky enough to be walking through the doorway as it came to a sudden close. Zaz kicked the door of the office open and picked her shots. Her first two targets were the riflemen who opened and fired in her direction with unbridled focus. Their fire was quickly silenced. Next, she aimed at the five remaining grunts, starting with the burliest ones. The largest of the group charged directly at her, taking three shots to the chest before showing signs of fatigue. He came just within arms reach of her before he flopped down on the ground at her feet. The remainder of the Grellians were dead on the floor with four more precision shots.

She turned her head toward the vent and climbed in. Looking up, there was a thirty-foot climb to the exit. The space inside was tight, but there was enough width to give Zaz a brace for her back while her legs pushed her upward. Everything in the moment moved gracefully like she had practiced it. Within seconds she reached the top of the vent and looked out of the cover vents. Grellians were piling up near the cargo doors, some standing there with typical confusion, others trying to bash them open. They were oblivious to anything else going around them. Zaz blasted the cover off the vent and pulled herself out of it. She flipped the switch on her gun to the "Fun" position and pointed it at the crowd of Grellians.

"Eat shit, morons." She yelled out to them.

With confused looks, they turned in the direction of Zaz only to see a bright purple ball of plasma arcing in their path. It erupted in contact with the ground and began to pull everything within the area into it. Zaz didn't stand to watch this time. Before the eruption even started, she was already headed up toward the base of the massive structure.

She reached the docking bay and saw only a handful of guards patrolling around. They didn't appear to be concerned with the commotion below. Instead they were focused on doing exactly as they were told, which was to watch Taric.

Dipping behind a stack of cargo, she waited until two of them began walking toward the structure's makeshift entrance. Then, stepping out from behind the crates, she fired three attentive shots at the remaining guards, dropping them quickly. Immediately after, she ran toward the cage where they were keeping Taric.

He jumped as she approached the corner but quickly realized who it was. "Ah, Zaz! Wha- what are you doing here?"

"I'm getting you the hell out of here."

He shook his head, "No, no, you must stop, Zavon. He's going to destroy the galaxy!" He said with an exasperated breath.

Zaz lifted her hands calmly, "Hey, it's alright. We've got P.A.T.R.O.L on the way. They'll take care of all this. But, we need to get you out of here." She broke the lock off the cage and swung the door open, grabbing his wrist.

He grabbed her arm with force and shook it, "No, Zaz. If you do not stop him now... What he has done with Garreth's work... Even P.A.T.R.O.L could not stop him."

Her eyes went from stiff and determined to soft and scared, "Oh god...what have I done?"

"It's not about what we have done, but what we will do. Save the galaxy, Zaz. Nothing else will matter."

Gritting her teeth, she gripped his hands tight, "Right. Where is he?"

"Follow where those guards were headed. There's a lift that runs to the peak. He's there finalizing the work that the Grellians can't."

"OK," she looked at where the guards had gone and then back at him, "Taric, what is it? What is this thing?"

"It's a planetary laser. He's been working on this for quite some time, but something about what Garreth created triggered him to move quickly. I'm sure you've seen what it can do... I'm afraid of what he's got planned for this...."

"Alright, I'll take care of it. Stay here. I'll come back for you."

He nodded, and Zaz took off toward the guards.

| 17 |

Saving the Galaxy

The two guards had just begun to make their patrol back toward Taric's cage when Zaz strolled up on them. One was skinny and walked with an air of authority. At the same time, the other was massive in comparison,casually handling a flux cannon like it was nothing. Zaz immediately recognized the pair of Grellians walking toward her like a flashback. It was the same two she met back at Bork's cantina. A welcome reunion, she thought to herself.

She casually leaned against the arched entryway, swinging her gun around her trigger finger. "Hey boys, long time no see. Now let's make this easy. Where's the bossman?"

They swung their guns up and pointed them at her with big grins. "It's not gonna matter where the bossman is. You ain't neva' gonna see him, cause we have guns now too!" the skinnier of the two said.

"You think that's going to make things better for you?"

She gave an encouraging shrug, "Look, tell me the quickest way to get to Zavon, and I'll let you both live, easy peasy!"

The brutish one gave a grunt of dissatisfaction, "No more talk!"

He took a thundering step forward and pulled the trigger on his canon. Without missing a beat, Zaz rolled forward and grabbed a loose panel of the scrap metal lying on the floor. Lifting it in front of her, the blast was deflected up into the ceiling. The explosion startled the two Grellians, giving Zaz enough time to swing her own gun around and put one between the eyes of the lummox. He fell with a thud, and Zaz dropped the panel, pointing her rifle at the smaller one.

"Now, like I said. Where's Zavon?"

His eyes wide, the Grellian dropped his weapon and pointed down the corridor they had come from. "The lift, it'll take you to him."

She glanced up and down at him, "Any others up there?"

He shook his head no, "Just the fodder boys."

"What the hell is a fodder boy?" She said with a confused look.

"They feed it, make it live." He said, pointing at the structure they were standing on. "Won't matter if you get there, though. Already too late. Gonna power on soon.

Zaz sneered at him and flicked her gun toward the exit ushering him to leave. She watched him go before turning and running toward the lift. It was just like the rest of the structure, crude and hastily put together. Stepping on, she saw a lever near the gate and pulled. The gate closed, and the lift began moving. It was smoother than she thought it would be given who put it together. As the lift continued, she began to wonder how well they constructed the laser. Taric's reaction earlier answered that question for her.

The lift came to a stop at the peak of the edifice. The air was thin and cold. Looking down, she realized just how tall and imposing it really was. The gate opened, and she walked into the opening in front of her.

The inside at this level starkly contrasted with the laser's lower levels and outer hull. Everything was intricately built and placed together. Wiring ran neatly and organized throughout the wire racks lining the walls. The walls were made from polished steel and created a near-perfect tube that pointed toward a star-filled space. The walkway she was on ran down the tube toward a large platform that housed a sophisticated coil system, the likes of which Zaz had never seen.

A large humming began to emanate from the platform, and suddenly the coils began to change from metallic silver to glowing red. Zaz quickly started running down the catwalk toward the platform. Heat began to radiate from the coils, and the humming sound was quickening. Zaz touched the base of the platform just as the entire structure lurched backward, throwing her to her knees. A large beam erupted from the system before quickly dissipating.

"Ah, well, if it isn't my honored guest." A familiar smooth drawl said.

Goosebumps covered Zaz's skin, but she attempted to keep her calm. "Hey Zavon, just thought I should see what all my hard work has created, ya' know?" She picked herself up and dusted off her pants. Across the terrace, Zaz saw the tall, slim, blue-skinned figure of Zavon Dash.

He tipped his wide-brimmed hat at her, "Well, I must say, I'm quite glad you decided to try and shoot your way out of my detention. It lead to quite the discovery." He gestured to the wall beside her.

Zaz glanced over and finally noticed the wall of Grellian bodies fused to the back of the coil system. A knot grew in her stomach and the sudden urge to vomit followed. She braced herself against the other wall, "Oh, god. Zavon, what have you done?"

He flourished his hand forward, "I've completed my life's work, and soon this pitiful excuse for a galaxy will finally bow down before its new ruler."

Zaz gave him a confused look, "New ruler? What are you on about? No one's going to bow down to you... You're just the leader of the Grellians. No one cares about you!"

"Ah, yes. The pathetic and witless Grellians that everyone came to underestimate. They're surprisingly resourceful, you know?" He began pacing back and forth, "After the Galactic Parliament refused to help them, following Trida Tech's destruction of their home planet, I decided they would be the perfect partners in my venture. Politics were never my thing, but science is where I flourished. Grellians made the perfect assistants. They never questioned me once. Not even now." A grin spread across his face.

"So why the big laser? How will this propel you to the galaxy's new ruler?" She said as she examined the platform.

"I feel it's quite simple. I'm going to destroy Iridia. So the galaxy can say goodbye to that damned parliament and P.A.R.O.L.E. Once they're gone, the people will need someone to lead them, and who better than me?"

Zaz shook her head in disbelief, "That all seems pretty hollow. I find it hard to believe that you've done all of this just to take control of the galaxy."

He scoffed, "Come now, Miss Moon. I know you've heard the mysterious tales of Zavon Dash. How I arrived from parts unknown. Took on the charitable task of employing the Grellians. Grew the outer rim trade routes, the same ones you have worked for the last ten years. How do you think I was able to accomplish all of that?"

She rolled her eyes, "I don't know. I figured you were clever and took advantage of a bunch of morons."

"It is because I am better than all of you, and I don't mean that condescendingly. I am simply born better than you because I am a God. Evolved on the very sun this galaxy orbits. Something the parliament never thought could exist. And now I bring you all freedom from the chains of imperialism!"

"Oh, you're insane. Got it." She chuckled.

"Mock me if you wish. You'll see shortly." He said with a dismissive wave turning away from her and walking toward a control panel.

Zaz immediately began to look around, searching for a way to disable the laser but found nothing. Looking up at the wall of infused Grellians, she realized there was only one way to stop the device from working. Pulling her gun around, she started shooting them, one after the other.

"STOP! WHAT ARE YOU DOING?" Zavon yelled from across the platform.

"I'm ending this!" She replied, continuing to shoot the Grellians.

Suddenly Zaz felt a sharp pain in her ribs, but she knew it

wasn't from breaking them this time. She dropped her pistol, falling to her knees, and grabbed her side, feeling a long, sharp metal shard sticking out. Zavon stood over her with a furious look on his face.

"I will not have my work ruined by an impudent space rat like you." He spat on the ground and slapped her across the face. "Now sit there and watch as I free this feeble galaxy of their suppressors."

Zavon picked up her pistol and threw it off the terrace. He strode back to the control panel and keyed in the coding to configure the laser. The laser began to hum as he walked toward the wall with a handful of dead Grellians slumped over. He reached into his trench coat and pulled out a small vial. Zaz knew immediately that it was a vial of nanites. She watched as he poured them onto his hand and placed it against the panel.

"I told you that I am a God. So it doesn't matter that you killed half of my battery. I alone contain enough energy to power this machine twenty times over." He reached out and touched the wall, the nanites quickly fusing his arm to it.

The hum became louder, and as Zaz continued to watch, she saw that Zavon began to glow. His blue skin turned lighter and brighter. At that moment, she realized he was telling the truth. Not that he was a God, but that he did evolve on the sun and that he was something she thought was only a fairy tale. Zavon Dash was an Iridite, creatures of the sun that were walking entities of power, and he was going to destroy Iridia.

Zavon bellowed a thundering yell, and radiation began flaring off of his body. The trench coat and large brimmed hat that once covered his body evaporated. Zaz shielded her eyes, and the laser charged up. A whirring sound originated from the controls, and Zavon glanced in their direction. At that moment, Zaz yanked the shard of metal from her side and leaped toward Zavon. The radiation from Zavon tore at Zaz's skin, but she pushed forward. With the sharpened side pointed down, Zaz lunged the shard directly into Zavon's arm and through it. His body returned to the rich blue it was before as he screamed, grabbing at his severed arm. Without hesitation, Zaz threw a stiff arm at his face knocking him unconscious.

She stood still, staring at nothing for a moment. Time was moving slowly, but she knew that was because of the blood she was losing. She looked down at Zavon, unconscious in front of her, and noticed a few more charred vials of nanites lying on the floor beside him. Scooping them off the floor, she walked toward the control panel, leaving a trail of blood behind her. She powered down the laser and found a comm system on the array.

Dialing into Jolene's station, she said, "Hey Jolene, Zaz here. I stopped him. Not sure I'll make it before help arrives, but can you make sure Garreth gets the rest of the nanites? I'll have them on me when you get here."

"We're on our way, darlin'. You just hang in there!" Jolene's warm voice came back.

Zaz smiled and put her back against the control panel, sliding down into a sitting position. After a couple minutes passed, she fell unconscious.

| 18 |

The Hero

"So, yeah. That pretty much sums it all up." Zaz said with a sigh of exasperation.

Terran Vass straightened himself to his original pointed posture, "I see." He pulled the recorder over and turned it off. " Well, I hate to say it but based on this information, I just don't see the Parliament giving you any leeway Miss Moon. Your actions were reckless, and despite the outcome, Helix tech isn't going to let this go, I'm afraid."

Zaz rolled her eyes, "Ugh, whatever. Guess that's what happens to heroes these days. By the way, thanks for getting me patched up on the flight over. Not sure you really needed to cuff me, though. Not like I was going anywhere."

"Standard protocol, Miss Moon."

"I told you, call me Zaz." She grinned.

A knock on the door caused both of their heads to look over. Terran answered the door and was greeted with a document pad. He examined the information and looked at the guard that had delivered it. His posture broke slightly before he caught himself and stiffened back up.

"Are you sure?" He asked authoritatively.

"Yes, sir. From the Parliament directly."

Captain Vass glanced over at Zaz and back at the guard and sighed, "Very well then." The door closed, and he sat back down in front of her. "It seems that the powers that be have, in all their infinite wisdom, agreed to let you go, free of charge."

Her grin became devilish, "Oh? You don't say, and why is that?"

He pinched the bridge of his nose and let out a heavy sigh. "It seems that your discovery of a species once thought a myth, as well as your assistance in the Atina Fleet's mission, has granted you an honorary pardon."

"Oh, wow, that sounds super fancy!" She said mockingly.

"And it seems that your business relationship with Garreth Tydol entitles you to insurance that covers damages related to your deliveries. Including that of Helix Industries."

Zaz's eyes widened, "Oh, now that is excellent information to have... So uh, how do I get out of here?"

Terran opened the door again, showing her the exit with a dejected look, "Last door on your right."

Kicking off the desk, Zaz jumped out of her chair and walked toward the door. "Thanks, Captain. It was a real blast." Then, patting him on the shoulder, Zaz strode down the hallway and out of the station.

THE END...

ABOUT THE AUTHOR

Introducing Tim, a fresh voice in the literary cosmos who is ready to embark on an interstellar storytelling odyssey. With a background steeped in the art of crafting captivating marketing messages, Tim now takes center stage as a first-time author, ready to ignite readers' imaginations with his debut work.

Tim's journey into the realm of writing began as a passion project, nurtured by countless hours spent crafting imaginative short stories and masterminding epic role-playing game campaigns. In 2020, a pivotal moment sparked a new chapter in his writing career, propelling him to take the leap into the realm of self-publishing. From that moment, the seeds of this gripping novella were sown.

Fueling Tim's creative fire is a love affair with sci-fi cinema that spans light-years. Inspired by the timeless allure of Star Wars and its universe, he channels his enthusiasm for the genre into his own narratives, infusing them with a thrilling sense of wonder and adventure. But it doesn't stop there—Tim's passion for exploration extends beyond the silver screen. As an avid gamer and dedicated tabletop role-playing enthusiast, he draws inspiration from immersive video game worlds and intricately woven board game sagas, enriching his storytelling palette.

In Tim's captivating novella, he weaves a tale that reminds us of the preciousness of life's fleeting moments. Through a cosmic lens, he unveils a powerful message: it's the vibrant characters, the bonds of friendship, and the tapestry of relationships that truly make our existence extraordinary. Tim's words transport readers to captivating dimensions, where they'll be enthralled by heart-pounding action, witty dialogue, and unexpected twists that keep the pages turning.

Join Tim on this exhilarating literary voyage as he unleashes his creative spirit and invites readers to embrace the remarkable people who color our lives. With his infectious enthusiasm and imaginative prowess, he reveals that the universe is brimming with endless possibilities—ones that are waiting to be explored, cherished, and shared.

Prepare for liftoff and let Tim's debut novella take you on an extraordinary journey—a cosmic adventure that reminds us of the beauty and significance of the connections we forge along the way.